GHOSTS OF
YESTERDAY

DAD,
HAPPY BIRTHDAY OLD MAN?
I'M GLAD I GET TO SEE
YOU ON YOUR SPEACIAL DAY.
ENJOY THESE STORIES. I LOVE YOU.

♡ EMILY AUTUMN

3/10/03

Other books by Jack Cady:

The Haunting of Hood Canal
The American Writer
The Night We Buried Road Dog
The Off Season
Street
Inagehi
The Sons of Noah
The Man Who Could Make Things Vanish
McDowell's Ghost
The Jonah Watch
Singleton
The Well
Tattoo
The Burning and Other Stories

GHOSTS OF YESTERDAY

Stories by Jack Cady

Night Shade Books
San Francisco & Portland

For Carol, as always

CONTENTS

THE LADY WITH THE
BLIND DOG

She may have once been a lady, and so Jill and I choose
to think of her that way. I was first to meet her. She
seemed a miserable old woman who tugged a panting
dog through crowded streets, beneath blue sky and sun.
We met during summer when light lay across San Francisco like the gaze of Mediterranean gods. Jill and I were,
and still are, warmed by that sun; but now sometimes
feel held in place; pinioned.

When Jill met her, Jill said, "She makes me feel so
old, and I'm not ready. Only the blush of the rose, that's
only what I want. I don't want to be old. I don't." Her
voice almost hysterical.

That was quite some years ago. Jill is now old, but
can't get accustomed.

The Lady grew no younger; but not a day older, either. The dog still pants, unchanged.

The dog is a mixture of small, fluffy breeds with white
fur, and with feet callused and clumsy. The callus comes
from a constant round of padding along sidewalks. The
nose is flat like a pug, and the eyes are pop-eyed like a
Boston bull terrier. The eyes vary; chalk white, fish-belly
white, dead white, and they contrast with the red tongue,
always panting.

It's got a red collar, too big for a dog that can't weigh more than five pounds. It's got a temper, because it will snap at anything or anybody. The lady drags it on a leash stout enough to hang a man. There are chew marks on the leash, but the dog's teeth are worn flat. It never barks. It never growls, or not exactly. It makes a low sound, a rumble, a noise that somehow sounds like fire racing before wind. If the dog actually growled, I think people would flee.

Flee from a five pound monster? Probably. With monsters, size doesn't matter much.

"Our monster," Jill says. "Does everybody have one, or are we just lucky?" She's still a lovely lady. The blush of the rose has long faded, but the high forehead has no more wrinkles than in her youth. Her hands remain lovely, her figure slim, and her neurosis only wild enough to make her interesting.

When young she wanted to be an actress, which is half of why we came to San Francisco. At the time the city owned a reputation for experimental theater.

The other half: I wanted to be a landscape architect drawing graceful lines of leaves across the world; make the world beautiful. I had other wants as well. I wanted to be warm. We were in Boston where outside-work is a frigid five-month sentence during winters. You have to let your hair grow to protect your neck. Your hands are never warm, nor your feet. I spent my last two winters there with a tree company, pruning and snow removal.

When we got to San Francisco I didn't even need to get a haircut; just walked into the office of the nearest landscape construction company, and walked out with a job. At the same time, in Cleveland and Chicago, there were riots and looting. In those days I paid little attention to the news. My attention focused on the job.

In the downtown financial district, where the old lady first showed up, there was a well-established pocket-park.

The park sort of dwelt between tall buildings. People from the offices took their lunches on good days. They sat on lush grass and chatted, chewed sandwiches, sipped thermos coffee, and for a few minutes quit pretending that what they did was especially important.

As the business district grew, and as more buildings rose, the park became crowded. My first assignment was foreman of construction for a new park. My crew and I built it right across the street.

The architect designed the place with seven little hills, because San Francisco is built on seven hills. It was a routine design, nothing exotic, but green and functional. Our machine operator piled and carved soil. A subcontractor put in sidewalks. My guys installed irrigation and pine trees, and then seeded grass. After which, I went sort of crazy.

It wasn't an ordinary job, or ordinary conditions; at least not to someone with experience. The irrigation heads were placed in a way that, with the touch of a button, I could light off enough water to cover seven little hills and better than an acre of ground; silver arcing flashes crashing above raw soil.

And, it was the middle of summer. Cloudless days. Overflooding sun. Grass seed down. What I did made no sense, except — ask any gardener.

Grass seed dies if it dries once wetted. A constant sheen of water is wanted. I made a bet with myself. I bet that I could bring that job in so fast it would go in the record books. And I did, from first water to first cutting in seven days.

Water crashing silver through sunlight, strong as creation, beautiful as hope. I dodged here and there, wet half the time while adjusting irrigation heads. Turn off the water, let the soil heat beneath that sun. When the first spot of gray showed surface dryness; time to light 'em off for another five minutes.

Crazy old lady. She first appeared on a sidewalk in the park across the street. From a distance she moved like a dark blotch against green grass, and beside loads of people dressed for business; gaily colored dresses, summer suits of tan.

The dog half-walked, was half-dragged beside her. The old bat could have allowed the dog to walk on grass, but she short-leashed it. The dog couldn't stray an inch. It had to walk on hot concrete. Even from across the street, you could tell it was blind.

The lady dressed witchery. Her darkish dress hung near shoe tops, thin ankles; dress of dark maroon but faded to sort of red — shabby where it almost touched her shoe tops. The dress looked made of velvet, and the lady wore a ragged fur jacket, but she shivered beneath that sun. Her face looked like someone or something had taken a normal human head and twisted it. Her lips sagged and could not quite close. Her face was smooth around the eyes, but it seemed like one eye rode a good bit higher than the other. Her face sagged everywhere else. Her eyes were closer to black than gray. Small slobber occasionally dripped.

"They wonder about you," she whispered. "All of them. They watch you scamper, and they wonder." Her voice sounded metrical as a harsh poem.

"You're gonna burn up in that coat," I told her. "You're gonna get heat stroke." Crazy old lady. I looked across at the other park, from which no one paid the least attention. "Nice dog. What's its name?"

She shivered. Beside her the dog panted. The eyes seemed to change in the sunlight, from milky to wheyish, sometimes marble-white. The dog did not rest on its haunches, or lie down; it never has. It is always ready to spring.

"Are you okay?" I asked. Sun already had me burned brown, and my hair bleached. Now the sun lay between my shoulders like a hot iron. The lady shivered. I thought she might pass out.

"Torment," she said, and I did not know whether she spoke of herself or the dog. "Don't come close.... Nothing wrong with his nose."

The dog's nose was crusted, the way dogs get in the last stages of distemper. Bald patches lay scabbed in the wavy fur. Its tail hung thin and ratlike.

I remember thinking she was cruel not to have the animal killed. Then I thought maybe the dog was her only companion, and she was so old.

Around us, I could feel the first stirring of life as seed germinated. It was like the soil began to breathe. Life, then death. Turmoil, then darkness. Regeneration, then life.

"Don't you mind them," she said. "And don't you worry. You can make the world beautiful. I've got my eye on you." She tugged at the leash. The dog snapped at air, snap, snap, clicks of flat teeth. White-popping eyes.

I watched her leave, dark ruby splotch against the gleaming white of the city. She walked less than a half block and then sort of faded. It didn't happen fast, and there were people going to and fro on the sidewalk. She might have stepped into a doorway, but that seemed un-likely. I told myself I wasn't scared. Later on, I told Jill I wasn't scared. What a liar.

I told Jill during one of our little dust-ups. We fussed at each other because of the job. She didn't understand why grass was important.

Seed hit the red stage in three days. The red stage is crucial. It's when the seed has to stay constantly wet. If you can bring it from red to green, and keep it green for thirty or forty hours, the job is home free.

What happened was, I parked at the job and slept in my car. I woke from time to time, like a mother with a new baby. Hit the irrigation for a couple of minutes, then go back to uneasy sleep. Jill spent nights at home, trying to persuade herself that I was not out with another woman. She tried to stay nailed in place, but paranoia got the best of her.

She wanted to be an actress, but what she needed was acting lessons. She showed up at the job around ten at night: a snazzy-looking young woman, riding a bus, then walking the empty streets of San Francisco; a young woman bearing sandwiches. Pretending love, and not paranoia.

"You didn't have to, but thanks." I actually sort of treasured the sandwiches, even if she was nuts. I could, back then, be as phony as she. Then I paused, realizing she was scared. If she was not scared, she would have checked me out from a distance, then gone back home.

"I'll give you a ride, then come back."

The old lady appeared beneath street lights as we climbed in the Ford. I wondered if the lady patrolled that park across the street. I wondered how somebody that old could constantly walk, day and night. The dog shone as a small white spot beneath street lights. The lady moved slow as befitted her age, but she dragged the dog most firmly. The leash tied them together, tighter, at the time, than Jill and I were tied. I started the car.

"Drive roundabout," Jill said. "Don't go the direction she went." Then she said, "Please."

"Problem?"

"I don't want to be old," she whispered. "There's stuff I got to do. Ingénue, that's me."

Jill was never little-girl pretty. She had the face and body to play Shakespeare's Portia, not some comic twinky. Her face and body are as far as matters ever went. She pretended she knew it all. She figured talent doesn't need training. Jill can pretend to perfection, but it's always Jill pretending. She never learned to act.

Driving her home, in that night long ago, it took less than a minute to find that she too had met the old lady. It happened on a deserted street; deserted because the San Francisco business district lay like a black and abandoned tomb after dark. Jill had seen the lady and dog from a block away. They crossed paths because who could imagine danger from an old lady and a tiny mutt?

"She told me not to worry," Jill whispered. "She said to examine my skills. What skills? I can type. She said she was keeping an eye on me." Jill's voice came as close to sounding 'little-girl' as I've ever heard. She was totally scared, dry-mouthed and spitless.

What I didn't tell Jill, or at least didn't tell her for some years, is that the old lady said, "Don't worry. I've got my eye on you," to lots of people. Mostly, she was ignored, which is the standard in San Francisco. The city is, or used to be, proud that people can be as weird as they want, as long as they don't cause trouble.

My grass came in (I thought of it as mine), and the maintenance crew arrived with lawn mowers. I left the park for other installation jobs, running as far north as San Rafael, and south to San Jose. The company landscaped freeways, power transfer stations, business and industrial parks, The Cow Palace, universities, and BART, the rapid transit system. Then, in three years, the company went broke. Too many Chiefs, not enough Indians.

And, during those years, all hell broke loose. Riots and burning in Atlanta and Boston, Buffalo and Cincinnati, Tampa, Newark, Detroit. The newspapers reported a war going on in the far east, but I had my own troubles.

Unemployment happened. I found myself back on the streets in autumn. Landscape outfits cut back against the coming winter rains. Jill worked as a temp secretary and started hanging out with little theatre groups. I looked for any kind of work.

It was a thin time, but had its points. I job-hunted

from early morning to mid-afternoon, then, discouraged, loafed. For the first time in a long time, I was able to watch what went on. I learned to like the scurrying of shoppers in the west end. I liked the mixtures of colors and languages and oriental faces; plus Irish and Italians, Russians, Hebrews, a sprinkling of Spaniards.

The old lady appeared one afternoon near the bandstand in Golden Gate Park. I saw her from a way off, saw mostly the white spot of dog, and faded velvet dress. I loitered on a park bench, like a bum in a two-bit movie. Sea gulls squawked overhead, circling, but they stayed away from her; or maybe away from the dog.

"Torment," I said when she approached. "He's looking well." I moved to one end of the bench, making space. "Take a break." Scared yes, but I was interested. Anything that can impress a seagull....

"He looks the same," she said, and she actually took a seat. I had the uncanny feeling that she was there, but really wasn't. I felt that if I touched her, my finger would go right through. Like, maybe, spectral.

The dog stood short-leashed, and two feet from my ankle. "Such a lovely city," she murmured. "Such a pretty day. By the time I'm free to know it...." She paused as the leash tightened, and the dog tried for my ankle. She held it most firmly. The dog rumbled, panted; red tongue, white fur, scabby and blind.

I felt sorry for her. She spent her days, even her nights, walking around tied to a dog that should be dead of old age. There had to be something better for her than that. "If you let him run, he couldn't go far."

"The last time he ran," she said, "quite a few ended in a graveyard." Her voice sounded honestly sad, like she honestly spoke the truth.

I didn't mind if she was crazy. After all, I lived with Jill who was nutsy. I wasn't all that bright myself; stupid enough to work, when I worked, at deadend jobs that offered only plants and trees as benefits. Plus, half of the people on the streets seemed screwy. One more Crazy didn't matter.

"He enjoys suicides and mayhem," she whispered, as much to herself as to me. "Decimation is his nature. Decimation is his right." She sat wrapped in the fur jacket, sitting in sunlight and shivering. A little slobber hung as a droplet in one corner of her mouth. "When he runs, people make fatal jumps. They destroy others, destroy things. They kill what they say they love." The dog stood on thin legs. It looked like it could hardly walk, leave alone run.

"I must go," she said. "I have my work." She stood. "You can weather hard times. I've got my eye on you. Don't worry."

At that time, in Los Angeles, people were scared because of something called the Tate-Bianca murders. It had something to do with cults. Whatever.

I got a job driving city bus. Half of the guys driving those things were splow-heads, freaks, junkies, jerk-offs; and generally on their way to rehab or a cemetery. The other half were guys worth knowing. I tooled bus for fifteen years.

For awhile I kept hunting something better. Took a couple of night classes at community college; agronomy and botany. Actually designed and installed a Japanese garden in the tiny yard in back of our apartment. Could have done more.

Should have done more. Could have been an architect. But, a day's shift of driving sends a guy home tired. The pay was okay, it became easier to work than think.

Jill hung out at little theater, helped paint sets. Caught an occasional walk on. Never really studied. She depended on a scant and untrained talent.

It came to me, as I wore out brakes by the truckload, that something magical happened in the streets of San

Francisco. Tons and tons of people, lots of whom didn't even speak English, managed to get along and not kill each other.

They fought traffic that ran like demented weapons. Hysteria should, and maybe did, lie just beneath the surface, but mass murder didn't happen.

What did happen is the skyline changed. The city grew upward, suburbs expanded, and craziness of a different sort lurked on every corner. Too many people, too much money, and too much desperation to make the rent. And, yet, no mass murder. Murder, when it happened, remained personal, husbands and wives, or jealous lovers.

In that time I saw the old lady twice, but I saw some other people first, because it turned out that the old lady was only one of several. On Geary Street, among lots of old men walking their dogs, there was one old man who had a three-legged mutt. It looked like a weiner dog crossed with a sick hamster. The man dressed in wool suit and top coat on the sunniest days. His face was cratered and twisted, the way sick men, and addicts, and alkies get in the last stages. He slowly limped in one direction while his dog limped in the other. They made a crooked pattern of movement along the sidewalks. One time, as I stopped to pick up passengers, I heard the guy say, "Chaos, stay!" The dog did not sit, but it stood motionless.

And there were other old men and women. I learned to spot them. Old people were pretty much everywhere, and lots of them had companion dogs. Most all of them were perfectly normal. Perfectly nice.

Occasionally, though, unusual ones showed up. Always with a mangy mutt. Always dressed against cold, as if the slightest San Francisco mist would blow right through them. For one three-month period I actually held my own investigation, kind of tracked them down.

One dog was named Despair. The other names were worse.

So I met the old lady two more times. The first time was in a wretched little park sandwiched between California Street and a nowhere lane of forgotten asphalt. Jill was with me, and it had been a lot of years since Jill met the old lady. Jill understood what I did not.

"She's not real. No one that old walks around. Dogs don't live this long. She's a hallucination." Sometimes Jill's brand of crazy comes up with truthful stuff. This time, her smooth forehead wrinkled with something that wasn't exactly fear, but surely wasn't confidence. Still, she tugged me forward. I tugged back. She won.

"Are you real?" she asked the lady. "If you are, then am I? Why are we here, and doing this?"

I expected Jill to ask after the Meaning of Life, but she must have missed a cue. Jill is narrow and leggy, very good-looking, and she stood hand on hip like a cowgirl about to grab a shootin' iron. Lousy acting. Jill was still Jill.

"I serve a sentence," the lady whispered, "but it's kind of you to ask." At her feet the dog seemed poised for attack.

"Sentence? Like in jail?"

"That's a fair description," the old lady said. She wiggled the leash, looked down at the dog, and tried to smile. Her face was so twisted the smile turned out crooked. "I keep Torment leashed. There's power in that, but not a power anybody would want."

"But are you real?" Jill can be a genuine pain when she sets her head on something.

"Torment is real," the old lady said. "Once in awhile he gets off leash. Perhaps you're still too young to understand."

At the time, Jill was pushing forty. Old enough to play Shakespearian tragedy. Unskilled though, and so she wasn't gonna.

"When he gets off-leash I get a year added to my sentence," the old lady said. "Don't ask how. I don't know."

"How long are you in for?" Dumb question, but I felt I had to say something before Jill stole the whole scene.

"In a few years the twentieth century will pass," the old lady murmured. "If he stays on leash for a few more years...." She seemed taken with a chill, or maybe she figured she'd said too much.

"Why?"

"You don't want to know," she told me. "If you ever do know, then you may walk for a century. She wiggled the leash. The dog clicked its worn teeth, made that fire-rushing noise.

"One does get weary," she whispered, "tired of being needed. And now we must go."

She moved away most slowly. I thought to follow. Jill stopped me. "Epiphany," she said, "don't screw up the dramatic moment." I didn't know what she meant, and neither did she. Or maybe she did. She seemed scared.

Something came between us after that. Jill grew remote. We still walked sunny streets. We still strolled the parks on Sundays. We still embraced, but distantly. I knew that a gulf was opening between us, partly because my dreams caused sadness.

I dreamed night after night of irrigation crashing white spume beneath sun. I dreamed of tall buildings, naked and needing greenery, ferns, trees. I dreamed I could fly, could cast growing things across bare landscapes, turn deserts into gardens.

I quit driving bus, and drove cabs. It came to me that I was no longer young. The little Japanese garden in the rear of our apartment turned scruffy. No matter how much attention I gave it, something went wrong. Somehow or other, my eyes had lost their ability to judge proportions. The garden looked like it stepped fresh from the pages of *Sunset* magazine, something rubber-stamped.

In other cities across the country there were riots, bombings of abortion clincs, assassinations. I found myself muttering, "Chaos must have gotten off leash." The minute I said that to myself, I knew it must be true.

And, almost right away, some guy proved to me it was true. The fare wanted a cab from airport to business district, and his destination stood near that park I'd landscaped so many years ago. A crippled old man led a three-legged wiener dog between green hills of grass. My passenger muttered to himself. I said "What?" He said, "How in hell did that man get here, all the way from Miami?"

"You're sure?"

"I'm not sure of much these days," the guy said, and he was grim. "But I'm damned sure I saw that man and mutt in Florida."

"Or else you saw a ghost?" I just suggested it; sort of had to suggest it.

"Could be," the guy said. "What the hell do I know?" He looked ahead, searching for his address, and became all business.

Jill decided that actors were troubled people, and directors were saints. She stopped the walkons, and turned motherly. Her little theater group depended on her for counsel, and for suggestions on set design.

Jill said, telling of the group, "If everyone would do exactly as I say, they would all be happy." ... quite a mouthful, but the group put up with it. They allowed her to direct a farce. It wasn't a good production, but it wasn't awful.

"You really shouldn't ask," the old lady told me on the last time we met. "I keep Torment leashed. I'm a protector of dreams."

She stood shivering beneath noonday sun, her fur jacket wrapped tightly over the velvet dress. Along the busy sidewalk people passed intent on business, or lunch, or a love affair... people intent on raising kids, or scoring a high; all the things that people do. The dog clicked its worn teeth.

"And those other dogs, Chaos, and Despair? Those old men?"

"They, too," she said. Those old men pay their debts. Sometimes they fail. Their charge, their creature, runs loose."

"Debts?"

"We pay for our failed dreams," she whispered. "Once in the long ago I wished to be a dancer. I suppose I did not want it enough to make it happen." Sorrow, like no sorrow I have yet known lay in that whisper. It was the sorrow of lost years, failed ambitions, paths taken because they were, if nothing else, easy enough, and practical. Sorrow.

"And so we rein in foul creatures. We try to protect the dreams of others." She tugged at the leash, turned away, and entered the hurrying crowd only to disappear like blown mist.

I'm not going to tell Jill about that. I'n not going to tell Jill that yesterday I saw Torment, still on leash. But this time an old man, dressed in thin robe beneath heavy greatcoat, was in charge. Our old lady's sentence has completed.

No, I won't put that kind of fear before Jill's eyes. It's bad enough that she frets over me these days, and there's not much she can do. She joins in a drink before dinner, or maybe a couple of them. They blunt whatever needs blunting.

Because no matter what I do, I know that one of these days an old man, or an old woman, will step into

my cab. They will have a creature named Sorrow on leash.
When they leave the cab, Sorrow will remain. So will the
leash.

Jeremiah

At the meeting of two secondary roads, Hell-Fer-Certain Church stands like faded rag-tags left over from a cosmic yard sale. This once quiet country church, with a single bell in the steeple, has virginal white paint decorated with psychedelic shades of pink and orange and green; those colors mixing with hard yellows and blues positive as bullhorns. For a short time in the past this abandoned church was used by a commune.

In the tower beside the cracked bell dangles a loudspeaker that once broadcast rock music, or called faithful flower-folk to seek renunciation of a world too weird for young imaginings. Then the speaker died, insulation burned away, the whole business one gigantic short circuit as sea wind wailed across the wires.

And the vivid paint, itself, faded before the wind and eternal rain that washes this northwest Washington coast. Those of us who once congregated at the church have dispersed, some to cemeteries to doze among worms, some to board rooms of corporations. And some, of course, have stayed in the neighborhood, too inept, or stoned, or unimaginative to leave; although in dark and mist-ridden hours we sometimes recall young dreams.

Then, lately, the church added one more perturbed

voice to its long history. A new preacher drifted here from dingy urban streets. In the uncut grass of the front yard a reader-board began carrying message. It advised passersby to atone, although around here folks show little in the way of serious transgression. They cheat at cards, sometimes, or drive drunk, or sleep with their neighbor's wives or husbands; and most shoot deer out of season. On the grand scale of things worth atoning, they don't have much to offer.

But the reader-board insisted that, without atonement, the wages of sin are one-way tickets to a medieval hell, ghastly, complete, and decorated with every anguish imagined by demonic zeal; seas of endless fire, the howl of demons, sacramental violence in the hands of an angry God.

And fire, we find — be it sacramental or not — has become part of our story.

On Sundays the new preacher stood in the doorway. Jeremiah is as faded as the faded paint on his church. His black suit and string tie are frayed, his white shirts are the only white shirts left in the county, and his sodbusting shoe tops are barely brushed by frayed cuffs of pants a bit too short, having been 'taken up' a time or two. He needed no loudspeaker or bullhorn as he stood preaching in the wind. When it comes to messages like "Woe Betide" Jeremiah had the appearance, vision, and voice of an old time prophet predicting celestial flames and wails of lost souls — no amplification needed.

......

There are, in this valley, some who view Jeremiah and sneer. A few others value Sunday morning services. Many are too busy or drunk to care. Some are outright displeased. Rather than tell all opinions about Jeremiah, or lack of them, a cross-section of comments by some of the valley's main players seems appropriate:

Mac, skinny, balding, and fiftyish, runs Mac's Bar and was first to see Jeremiah arrive: "As long as he stays on his side of the road I treasure the jerk. There's a certain amusement factor."

Debbie, who is an artist, a barfly, a fading beauty, and thoughtful: "I've tried a lot of this-and-that in my time, but I never molested a preacher. Have I been missing something?"

Pop, gray and wiry and always sober, is a small-time pool and poker hustler: "Seems like he works purty hard for blamed little in the collection plate."

Sarah's religious beliefs, like her tie-dyed clothes, have followed currents of popular style. Through the years she has embraced Hari Krishna, the Pope, Buddha, Sidhartha, Mohammed, and Karl Jung, while mostly wearing mother Hubbard styles. "It's the Lord's blessing has sent Jeremiah to us. Praise the Lord. Praise him!"

......

Not many people live here anymore. One of the secondary roads that meet at the church corner leads up from the sea. At the harbor are abandoned docks and fishing sheds where ghosts drift through fog-ridden afternoons. The buildings are huge, like a town abandoned by giants. Ghosts glide through mist, whisper like voices of mist, fade into mist when approached. We've gotten used to them. The ghosts threaten no one, except they seem so sad, the sadness of ghosts.

The other road leads through a flat valley where empty farmhouses lean into sea winds that rumble from the western coast. The houses are ramshackle. Shakes on roofs have blown away, and broken windows welcome the scouring wind. They are, themselves, ghosts; ghost houses that daily remind us of mournful matters; symbols of abandonment and failed plans.

What was once a valley of small dairy farms has been purchased farm-by-farm, and built into one huge corporation farm worked by only a few men. Our farms once had names: River View, Heather Hill, and a dozen others.

Now, cattle are bred, no longer for milk, but as blocks of meat. The valley has become a source of supply for a hamburger kingdom, a franchise that ships product to fast food joints in Seattle, Yokohama, and maybe, even, Beirut. The cattle, well adapted to wind that roughs their heavy coats, grow thick on hormones and valley grass. Then they are trucked to slaughter.

Across the road from Hell-Fer-Certain stands an old post office little larger than a postage stamp. Weathered benches in front of the post office serve loafers, or people waiting for a bus to Seattle. A country store stands next to the post office. Mac's Bar stands next the store. If you visit the bar on a Saturday or Sunday night you'll swear this valley holds every old pickup truck in the world. People congregate at the bar to forget they are survivors of a failed place. No one farms anymore. No one fishes.

One important thing happens on Sunday night, and it draws the Sunday crowd. Cattle get restless as headlights and marker lights of trucks appear on two-lane macadam. The trucks, twenty or more, arrive in groups of two or three. They pull possum-belly trailers built like double-deckers so as to haul more beef. The truckers will not load live cattle until Monday morning, but by Sunday night the cattle already know something stinks. The beasts become uneasy. The cattle, bred for meat and not for brains, still have survival instincts. The herds cluster together, each beast jostling toward the middle of the herd where there is an illusion of safety. Bawling carries on the winds. The entire valley fills with sounds of terror.

Folks swear it's Jeremiah's preaching riles the cattle, but we know it isn't so. As trucks roll in, Sunday nights turn into Jeremiah's busy time. He stands before Hell-Fer-Certain and preaches above the wind. His string tie flutters like a banner, and his white and uncut hair is whirled by wind that carries the bawling of bovine fear.

With no place to go, and a twelve hour layover, truck drivers drift to the bar and buy rounds. They're good enough lads, but they have steady employment and that gets resented. They generally come through the doorway of Mac's bent like fishhooks beneath the flood of prophecy coming from across the road. Jeremiah puts the fear of God in them. Plus, truck driving builds a mighty thirst in a man. It's that combination causes them to stand so many drinks.

......

This, then, is the place we live. It is not the best place, not the worst, but it's ours; a small and slightly drunken spot on the Lord's green earth. It was never, until Jeremiah and Mac got into it, a place where anything titanic seemed likely. Then Jeremiah confounded Mac's hopes. He crossed the road.

......

It began on one of those rare August afternoons when mist blows away, sun covers the valley grass, and hides of cattle turn glossy with light. The macadam road dries from wet black to luminous gray. A few early drinkers stay away from Mac's, vowing not to get fuzzy until the return of ugly weather.

Mac busied himself stocking beer cases behind his polished oak bar. Polished mirrors behind the bar reflected a clutter of chairs and tables around a small dance floor. The mirrors pictured colorful beer signs, brushed pool tables, dart boards, and restroom doors that in early afternoons stand open to air out the stench of disinfectant. Either a reflection in the mirrors, or a silhouette in the sun-brightened doorway caused Mac to look up.

"Praise the Lord," said the silhouette. Then Jeremiah moved out of sunlight and into the shadow of the bar.

"All I needed," Mac said as if talking to himself, "was…" and he squinted at Jeremiah, "this," and he squinted harder. Mac's balding dome shone like a small light in the shadowed bar. Although he's thin, he's muscular. At the time most of the working muscles were in his jaw. "You're a bad dream," Mac told Jeremiah. "You're the butt end of a bad joke. You're turnip pie. You're first cousin to a used-car salesman, and what's worse, you're in my bar."

Jeremiah looked around the joint which stood empty except for Debbie, the artist-barfly. Debbie looked Jeremiah over with her blue and smiling eyes, brushed long hair back with one hand, and gave a practiced and seductive smile that went nowhere; although it would have worked on a truck driver.

"A customer is a customer," Jeremiah said, and he did not sound particularly righteous. "And it appears that you could use one." He stepped to the bar like a man with experience. "Soft drink," he said. "Water chaser." Seen beneath bar light, Jeremiah turned from a cartoon preacher into a real person. His face looked older than his body. His hair, not silver but white, hung beside wrinkled cheeks, pouchy eyelids, and a mouth that sagged a little on the right side; a mouth that had preached too many adjectives, or else the mouth of a man who had suffered a slight stroke. He looked at Debbie. "A woman as well found as yourself could make a success if she cleaned up her act." Jeremiah commandeered a barstool, pushed a dollar onto the bar, and sat.

"You want something," Mac told him. "What?"

"We'll get to it," Jeremiah said, "and for your own good I will shortly get to you." He slowly turned to look over the bar. "It will be a quiet afternoon." Beyond the windows a beat-up pickup pulled away from the post office. Across the road Hell-Fer-Certain Church stood in faded psychedelic colors.

"I believe in evolution," Debbie said, her interest suddenly piqued.

"Who doesn't," Jeremiah told her, "except that it didn't produce humans. It only produced Charles Darwin. You may wish to think about that."

Debbie, thoroughly confused, now found herself thoroughly fascinated. She tried to think.

Mac, on the other hand, was not confused. After all, Mac is a bartender. "You talk like a man who is sane," he told Jeremiah, "so what's your hustle?" Mac looked through the front windows at the church. He seemed remembering the loud prophecy, the dogmatic hollering, the Sunday nights of wind and truck engines and sermons. "You don't talk the way you should." Mac's voice sounded lame.

It's a problem preachers have," Jeremiah told him. "The words we use are old, timeworn, water-smooth, and even, sometimes, decapitated. Our traditions are ancient, as are the symbols; crosses and lambs and towers of wrath. Plus, in today's world the volume on everything has been cranked higher. Would you pay attention to a quietly delivered message?"

Mac hesitated, wiped the counter with a bar rag, and seemed to remember younger days, days when people actually thought that they were thinking. "You just busted your own argument," Mac said. "I never paid attention before, but I'm hearing you now."

"In that case," Jeremiah told him, "we may proceed

with your salvation, and possibly my own." His voice sounded firm, advisory, nearly scolding.

Medieval hells of fire and brimstone, according to Jeremiah, were problematic ("I honor the tradition.") but Hell, itself, was certain, either in this world or the next. "All versions of hell get boring, because even anguish wears out sooner or later. I care nothing for it."

Debbie looked at her small glass of chablis, pushed it two or three inches away from her, and sat more sad than confused. Debbie is not a bad artist, and she might have been great. These days she paints cute pictures for sale to tourists. Things happen. Life happens.

"Don't get me started talkin'." Mac's tone of voice said the opposite of his words. Mac used to be a thinker, but few abstractions ever make it to a bar. Bartending causes rust on the brain.

"Which is why my main interest is atonement, thus redemption." Jeremiah sipped at his soft drink, looked at the label on the can, and gave an honest but crooked grin from his sagging mouth. "This stuff is not exactly sacramental."

"It's such a pretty day," Debbie said, "it's such a pretty day." She retrieved her small purse from the bar, walked to the doorway and stood framed in sunlight. Then she stepped into sunlight. She walked away, not briskly, but like one enchanted by a stroll in the sun.

"Handsome woman," said Jeremiah.

"Lost customer," said Mac.

"We'll speak again, and soon," Jeremiah promised. "Between then and now you may wish to ponder a question. How many differences, if any, are there between a preacher and a bartender." He stood, gave a backward wave as he walked to the doorway, and stepped into sunlight. His shabby suit and clodhopper shoes made him look like a distinguished bum, or an itinerant living on the bare edge of respectability.

......

The fabulous weather did not last. Mist rolled in from the coast. It was followed by rain. Hides of cattle turned glossy, and rain puddled in the churchyard of Hell-Fer-Certain. On next Sunday night, as trucks rolled in, Jeremiah performed like a champion, but with a different message. Anyone who paid the least attention understood that new images entered his calls for atonement. Instead of talking about lambs, he spoke of cattle. When speaking of heaven he no longer pictured streets of gold, but streets of opportunity. The image of the cross gave way to an image of the morning star. Hardly anyone gave two snips about images, but later on we would figure Jeremiah made changes in order to get Mac's attention.

And through the week, and through the next, it was Mac who changed the most, because (though no one knew it at the time) Mac tried to answer Jeremiah's question.

......

A good bartender is a precious sight, and Mac was always good. His instincts were quick, accurate, nearly catlike. He knew when to be smart-mouthed, when to be glib, and when to be thoughtful. He never lost control of the bar, but now he went beyond control and even directed entertainment.

If bar talk slowed, or the pool tables stood empty, Mac resembled a school teacher introducing new subjects. Instead of baseball, used truck parts, and cattle, we found ourselves cussing and discussing local Indian legends. We talked about the fall of empires, Roman and American. We quibbled over histories of Franklin Roosevelt and Henry Ford. In only two little weeks Mac's Bar turned into an interesting place to congregate, and not simply a place to get stewed.

Conversation improved but beer-drinking slowed. Mac ran a highly enhanced bar, but made less money. For those who know him well, Mac seemed slightly confused but almost happy. Since no one around here has been really happy for a long, long time, we were confused as well.

Meanwhile, gray day followed gray day and life went on as usual. On the coast, mist cloaked the broken wharves, warehouses. and abandoned fish cannery. Ghosts whispered through mist, nearly indistinguishable from mist; we thought them ghosts of fishermen lost at sea, ghosts of fishing boats long drowned.   Thus, from the coast to the fields, memories of work and order and dreams lay as sprawled as wreckage.

Those ghosts of the land, the abandoned houses, leaned before wind and seemed ready not to shriek, but groan. Cattle lined the fences beside the road. As they appeared through mist, the cattle looked ghostly; silvered black hides, pale white faces, bovine stares toward us, and toward the road that would shortly carry them to slaughter.

Then, on a Saturday afternoon when baseball should have been the topic, Mac looked across the bar, across to Hell-Fer-Certain, and said "What does he mean by atonement?"

"It's being sorry for screw-ups." Pop, our local hustler, leaned against the end of the bar nearest the pool tables. As afternoon progressed, and as beer built confidence among customers, one or another booze-hound would challenge Pop to dollar-a-game. Pop would clean the guy's clock, and his wallet. For the moment, though,

Pop was free to talk. He is a short, graying man, usually taciturn.

"It's more than that," Debbie said. "I can feel sorry for screw-ups any old time I want." She sipped at her wine. Her eyes squinched a little, and sorrow entered her voice. "Come to think of it, I usually want. Sorry most days...." She realized she was saying too much. She saw her reflection in the bar mirror, smoothed her hair with one hand, smoothed wrinkles on the sleeve of her blouse with the other.

"It's recognizing that you're out of sync with the universe." Sarah, granny-skirts and all, attends Mac's Bar on Saturday afternoons. She would be happier in a sewing circle or a book discussion group, but she doesn't own a sewing machine and we don't have a library.

"Ninety days for drunk-and-disorderly. That's atonement." Pop looked down the bar where sat at least three customers who knew all about doing ninety days. "I rest my case."

"That's only punishment," Debbie whispered. Almost no one heard her.

......

Jeremiah next appeared at ten a.m. on a rainy Monday. Truck engines roared as truckers slowed for the intersection of roads, then caught a gear and started building revs. The possum-belly trailers were crowded with living beef standing silent as ghosts, the animals packed together and intimidated; the trucks rolling purgatories for beasts.

Mac and Sarah and Debbie opened the bar. Or rather, Mac opened the bar while Sarah made morning coffee and Debbie loafed. Mac brushed pool tables and cleaned rest rooms. Sarah drank coffee and watched the road. Sarah, who is nobody's mother, looks like she would do

for the sainted mother of us all. Her face is sweet, her
hair hangs in long braids, her figure is slightly dumpy.
Her hands are workworn because she lives by cleaning
houses of corporation people. If Sarah has a problem,
and Sarah does, it's because she's a sucker for any new
trend. She keeps ideas the way other people keep goldfish. Like goldfish, the ideas swim in all directions.

When Jeremiah entered the bar, rain glistened on his
black suit and dripped from ends of his white hair.
Wrinkles in his face looked like channels for rain. He
sniffed the morning smells of the bar, stale tobacco, the
stench of disinfectant. The smell of fresh coffee seemed
to draw Jeremiah. He sat beside Sarah who was, at least
for the moment, one of his parishioners.

"Praise the Lord," said Sarah.

"You got that right." Jeremiah gave a couple of sniffs
and asked for coffee. He hunched above his coffee cup.
His black suit made him look like a raven regarding road-
kill. "Although," he said to Sarah, "if we must unceas-
ingly praise the Lord, does that mean the Lord has an
inferiority complex?   If the Lord needs constant praise
we may be dealing with a major case of insecurity."

Mac used a narrow broom to sweep between bar and
barstools. Jeremiah's question stopped him. He shook
his head. "I got to wonder whose side you're on?"

"I like you more positive." Sarah's voice did not
tremble, but she seemed alarmed. "The Lord is supposed to let people feel safe, and stuff... like, no mystery stuff."

"Thank God for mysteries." Jeremiah's voice
sounded nebulous as mist, although his words did not.
"Life without mystery would be life without dreams. The
universe would be dull indeed." Outside, at the intersection of roads, a truck engine roared as its driver revved,
then caught a higher gear.

"For instance," and Jeremiah looked at Mac, not Sa-

rah or Debbie, "do cattle dream? Does a young heifer
or steer muse beyond that next mouthful of grass? Are
there great cattle-questions? Better yet, are there herd
dreams? Does the herd graze according to music tuned
only to bovine ears?" Jeremiah's voice seemed not exactly sad, but he certainly was not joking.

"And do ghosts dream? Jeremiah looked into mist,
at the road that leads down to the sea. "A ghost may
actually be a dream. After someone dies, maybe a leftover dream stands up and walks."

"Quit scaring me," Sarah whispered. She raised workworn hands to cover her ears.

"I hope to scare you, because faith may not be as
productive as doubt. Doubt asks questions and faith does
not." Jeremiah's voice was not kind. He paused. "Is
there some dread realm where human dreams and the
dreams of cattle are appreciably the same?" He looked
across the road at Hell-Fer-Certain. "If so, what does
that say about all of us?"

At the time Sarah didn't get it, and Mac didn't either.
Knowing Mac, though, it was a lead-pipe cinch he'd catch
on sooner or later. He leaned against the bar. "Bartend-
ers and preachers have a lot going," he told Jeremiah.
"Both have something to sell, both exercise control over
others, both serve as handy ears for the confessions of
sinners." Mac grinned like a naughty three-year-old.
"Both flip a certain amount of bull, and what they sell
wears off after a good night's sleep."

"I'd fault your logic if it was worth my time."
Jeremiah pushed his coffee away. "Also, I asked about
difference, not similarity."

"My mistake." Mac sounded like a ten-year-old kid
caught stealing nickels.

"Meanwhile, suppose a ghost really is a leftover
dream?" Jeremiah stood, stretched, looked through the
windows at mist and rain. Then he looked at Mac with

distaste, like a man regarding a favorite nephew arrested on a burglary rap. "You can think more clearly than you have."

"You know it," Mac said, "and I know it."

"When I was young," Jeremiah told him, "I wanted to change the world... wanted to make things better... figured to find a cure for common hatreds, ignorance, wanted to defeat war... prejudice...." He seemed as puzzled as Mac. He looked across the road at the fading colors of Hell-Fer-Certain. When he left the bar he walked slower than usual.

......

Atonement became the name of our game. Redemption became more than a word in a sermon. Our problem came because we didn't know what needed atoning. If anybody needed redemption it couldn't happen until we figured out our original foul-up.

But anyone with brains could see that Jeremiah made a bold if harsh play for the heart and soul of one man, Mac. Jeremiah seemed old as king Solomon, at least in experience, and maybe as wise. Being old, he knew he had little time left. What he'd said about wanting to change the world told us he wasn't fooling when he talked about dreams. We supposed if he couldn't change the world, he figured to change one man.

And, if Mac made less money, our local hustler, Pop, made more. As the bar became a place for interesting topics, guys stayed sober, longer. Pop enjoyed a surge of prosperity because a good hustle depends on the full attention of the guy being hustled. Sober guys have longer attention spans. It was during a lull in sober conversation that an awful thing happened.

On a fog-bound afternoon when headlights on the road appeared as silver discs, and as fog muffled the sound of engines, Mac absent-mindedly drew a beer. He set it before a customer, and muttered to himself, "He's trying to figure out what happens when dreams fizzle...the death of dreams...."

Only Pop and Debbie heard. Debbie touched her wine glass, gave a dry little sob, and sat silent. Pop looked at Debbie, then at Mac. "You'd better not lay that one on the table," he whispered. "It will empty out the joint."

Mac emptied the bar, anyway. During the next hour he grew completely silent, then surly. If he was angry at himself and taking it out on customers, or his bar, or the universe, or on Jeremiah, no one could say. All we knew is that Mac was not jolly. As afternoon misted toward evening, customers stepped through the doorway into mist. By happy hour only Pop and Debbie remained. Bar neon glowed through mist like a token of sorrow, or like the subdued symbol of a small and unimportant corner of Hell.

"Everybody had big plans at one time or other." Pop murmured this, more to himself than to Debbie or Mac. "Time was when I didn't make a living with a pool cue." He looked at Mac in a kindly way, a way no one expects to see in a pool hustler. "We're gettin' old," Pop told Mac. "I guess we expected more...." He looked around the bar, at twirly beer lights and the green felt of pool tables. "...didn't expect more of the world, maybe. Expected more of ourselves."

"I'm headed home," Debbie whispered. "Art is not an illusion. I used to know that." She shrugged into her jacket and looked at the men. "Pay no attention. I don't understand it, either."

......

Fire struck our land during early morning hours. It drank deeply of wind, flared and flamed through mist like a maddened imp squalling in the middle of fields. It blasted the farmhouse of Indian Hill Farm.

Indian Hill's house stood ramshackle and wrecked a thousand yards from the road. As the first touch of dawn moved grayly above fields, fire towered and blew sideways, tongues of flame lapping at mist. Mist blew into the flames, mixed with flames, and steam exhaled from the very mouth of fire. Wind carried the fire, and fire flamed ascendent above wet fields. By full dawn, Indian Hill farmhouse lay as embers beneath a steady morning rain.

That first fire saddened us. Bar talk remembered people who once owned Indian Hill, their sons, daughters, cousins; even the name of their collie-shepherd mix, once known as the best cattle-herding dog in the valley. Bar talk remembered August days of cutting or baling hay, or of trucks pulling silver-colored tank trailers, making milk pick-ups at each valley farm. A drunk wrote "I miss you so goodam much," on the wall of the men's can, but Mac painted it over right away.

The cattle corporation uses the old barns to store equipment, even though the farmhouses are abandoned. The corporation brought in a bulldozer, cleaned up the burn site, and seeded it with grass. The bulldozer knocked down outbuildings. The old barn stood solitary in the middle of fields. It seemed a testament to memories.

The second fire took the house of Valley View Farm which stood behind a stubby lane, and up a little rise. That house had become a fearful thing. Because of the short lane, and the rise, the house brooded above the road like a specter. It was larger than most farmhouses, and two fanlights had once looked toward the road like colorful eyes. With abandonment the glass had been broken. The eyes stared toward the road, hollow as eyes of the blind.

This second fire was hard for us to talk away, think away, or drink away. It continued to flame in the minds of those who saw it (and most everyone did) long after rain washed ashes down the rise. The fire began just after nightfall on a Tuesday when the valley stood empty of tractor-trailers, of truckers, and reduced by some few hundred cattle. As fire towered above the road, pickups pulled to the side, parked, and people talked or stared. Mist once more blew into flames, turned to steam, and steam blew across the road and into our faces. The stench of burning carried in the mist, but something worse walked to us.

Cattle were in the fields. Against all nature, the cattle drifted toward the fire. The herd formed a semi-circle in the wind-blown mist. White faces of cattle stared through mist, were reddened by reflections from the fire. The cattle stared not at fire, but stared in ghostly illumination at the road where we stood helpless to affect events, and watched; where we spoke excitedly, or with sadness, or, with but a murmur. The cattle seemed to stand as witness to our lives, their eyes blank as the blind eyes of the dying house.

......

The corporation bulldozed, seeded, and called the sheriff. One fire might be accidental. Two fires spelled arson. The sheriff went through motions, but couldn't see the point. After all, the houses were worthless.

......

"It's a trick question," Mac confided to Debbie on one of those afternoons when wind drops and fog gathers thick enough to hinder traffic. Across the road Hell-Fer-Certain stood in the fog like a ghost. "The differ-

ence between a bartender and a preacher is no difference at all."

"Because?"

"Because jobs have nothing to do with the basic guy."
Mac looked around his bar like he saw it for the first
time. "That preacher is not a beat-up church, and this
bartender is not a bar. You got it?"

"If you came to that smart an answer," Debbie told
him, "then it wasn't a trick question."

If Mac had changed, and if Jeremiah was using different images, Debbie changed as well. Although she
told no one, images of fire occupied her, as did sadness.
"There's a word called 'expiation,' " she said in a low
voice. "I think we'll learn about it."

The third fire took Heather Hill Farm, and the fourth
took River View. By then August was long past, September waning, as fall rains began in earnest. The valley
filled with flame and steam. Cattle now grazed nearer
the road, stood looking across fences in that dumb, animal manner that seems asking for explanation.

Then, on a night when the sky seemed to seep absolute darkness, as well as seeping rain, Debbie trudged
toward the bar. Throughout the valley, as fires continued, sadness had become not only ordinary but a custom. We did not understand that it was not simply a few
old houses being burned away. Symbolically, flame engulfed our history. People headed to the bar where night
could not be defeated, but could be allayed. Neon signs
colored our night world. Cone-lights above pool tables
suggested focus and illumination. As Debbie passed the
reader-board in front of Hell-Fer-Certain she sensed
movement in the darkness. She gave a small, involun-
tary gasp.

"It's only me." Mac's voice sounded controlled, but
fearful. "Pop is running the joint for an hour or two."

"You're standing in rain before a church that drives

you nuts. Plus you've been acting spooky. Are you the arsonist?" Debbie hesitated, thought about fires and Mac's whereabouts. "You couldn't be unless you're setting them with a timer. You were behind the bar for two fires out of four."

Mac made a vague motion toward the church. "He is," Mac said.

"For the love of God." Jeremiah's voice came from darkness before the church. "For other loves as well."

"You're helping him" Debbie asked Mac. She felt for a moment that she should flee. "What are you doing out here if you're not helping him?"

"Because I thought I liked the guy. Because I'm sick-a selling beer. Because it isn't raining inside… how the hell do I know…." Mac's voice turned apologetic. "…sorry … I'm not sure why I'm here, but I am sure that hell is about to start popping. Look west."

Debbie turned. "You guys are scaring me. You are." In the west, like beginning sunset, a slight glow of orange showed at docks and cannery. "Mass fire, massive," Debbie whispered to herself. "If any of that goes, all of it goes."

"No water down there except what's in the ocean." Mac turned to where Jeremiah stood in darkness. "I reckon this is supposed to mean something?"

"I reckon it does." Jeremiah's voice did not sound preacherly, but grim. "Or maybe it's just a reckoning."

"Why are you doing this?" Debbie sensed Jeremiah's presence but could not find him in the darkness. Rain patted on her hooded parka. It puddled at her feet. "Everybody was getting by," she said. "Things aren't great but we were making it." She watched as the orange glow increased. "I won't cop on you," she whispered to Jeremiah, "or at least I guess I won't. But, you'd do well to have an explanation." She turned to Mac. "Everybody will be going down there pretty quick. Drive me."

Mac stood quiet, a man afraid, or maybe only indecisive. Debbie took his arm. She turned toward the darkness before the church. "Go ahead and tell me this is the will of the Lord," Debbie said to Jeremiah. "Then I'll know you're nuts." She walked toward Mac's pickup.

"Redemption by fire." Jeremiah's harsh whisper came from shadows before the church. "I don't think the Lord has much to do with it. You're an artist. Figure it out."

......

Immense fires, fires as big as cities burning, cast heat so huge they must warm the toes of heaven. Lesser fires, like the burning of a way of life, are localized, thus more spectacular.

By the time Mac and Debbie arrived, fire already covered docks and rose into the night through the roofs of warehouses. Sounds of burning, the crash of timbers, the roar of volcanic updrafts silenced the sounds of seawind and surf. Fire moved toward the enormous cannery as heat melted asphalt on the road between warehouses. When the road began to burn, a stench of petroleum mixed with dry smells of woodsmoke from flaming walls and floors; this while rain wept and blew across the scene, sizzled, pattered through mist.

Mac and Debbie stood halfway down a hill leading to the cannery. Heat coasted up the side of the hill and stopped their advance. Behind them, cresting the hill, headlights of old pickups pointed toward the fire as people arrived, the beams of light swallowed by fire. Firelight rose toward the scud of low-flying clouds, and black smoke crisscrossed through the light as heat mixed and churned the winds. As more and more people arrived headlights were switched off. People milled, clustered together, sought an illusion of unity, of safety. Fire swept into the broken doors of the cannery. Fire illuminated faces in the crowd. Firelight glowed orange on cheeks and hands. It glossed clothing with a sheen of red. Fire caused shadows, made eyes seem like hollows of night.

"Is this expiation?" Debbie whispered beneath the roar of fire. She watched as flame burst through the high roof of the cannery. Then, because it seemed nothing so awful could be focus for good, she looked away, then gasped. She tried to turn, tried to look back up the hill, or at the wet and weeping heavens, or anywhere except where her gaze finally was forced to focus.

On the periphery of the fire vague movement began in blowing mist. At first the movement seemed only swirls of mist, then shapes began to coalesce. Shapes drifted like unimportant murmurs. Mist blew among them, seemed to offer substance, and the shapes became human figures drifting toward fire, unhesitating, herd-like and passive; not, after all, only the ghosts of fishermen drowned, but the ghosts of dreams summoned to the burning; dreams that like threatened beasts gave final screams, then fell into mute acceptance.

...and Debbie saw a young Mac bouncing a basketball while coaching kids, and a young Jeremiah standing before a mission school. Mostly, though, she saw a young woman sitting before canvas, saw the turn of a young wrist properly pointing a brush, sensing the depth of colors in the palette, saw a young woman alive with the high dreams of art; then watched the diminishing form of that young and lovely woman, a woman aspiring to creation, drift slowly, inexorably, to disappear into the roar of flames.

"I think," said Mac in a voice too husky to come from anything but tears, "that it's time to get the hell out."

"And I think, said Debbie, "that your expression is apt. But I'm not sure I like you anymore. Go back without me. I'll catch a ride." She managed to control her voice.

......

Climax and anti-climax. Fire swept across the scene in fountains and waves. When the cannery roof fell machinery glowed red. Water pipes and steam pipes twisted, boilers stood like the crimson cauldrons of medieval hell, and people gradually stopped exclaiming, because nothing, it seems, can be remarkable forever. People climbed in their trucks, turned around, and told themselves and each other that what they really needed was a drink. The show was over, the festivities ended, a way of life had passed and no one even knew it.

Debbie, riding four-to-a-cab in a rickety pickup, looked beyond headlights and into mist. She felt slugged in the stomach. A glow stood in the sky.

......

To those who arrived from the destruction of the cannery, Hell-Fer-Certain Church burned as an afterthought. Flame lighted the inside of the church, and stained glass windows pictured scenes from Bible stories. Stained glass gradually fell away as heat melted lead, turned glass to powder when fire burst through to rise along the outside of the building. Psychedelic colors of pink and orange and green twisted beneath flame, turned brown, turned gray, and fell to ash. Fire roared to the top of the steeple where wind caused it to wave as a hellish flag. When the cracked bell and the broken loudspeaker fell from the steeple, only Debbie gave it more than passing thought.

As emotionally exhausted people drifted toward the bar, Debbie found she did not want a drink, did not want company, but did want to wring an explanation out of

Jeremiah. And, Jeremiah, it turned out, was not to be found.

Debbie looked toward Mac's bar, saw the glow of barlight, heard the loud voices of people with little information and large opinions. She turned back to the church and watched the last flames die to yellow flickers above coals. The flames licked feebly at mist, and Debbie became conscious that in the fields beyond Hell-Fer-Certain, herds lined the fences; cattle white-faced, ghostly in the illumination from dying flames, and mute.

......

We woke, next day, bewildered. Dullness spread across the valley. It invaded our lives, or rather, seeped into our lives. We lived in a place where dreams had died, a world of rain and cattle and embers. It was a world stripped of sense, stripped even of ghosts, and we began to understand that hell need not be spectacular, only dull. At least that seemed true.

Debbie watched, wept, thought, and recorded in her journal this history of our destroyed world. With the eyes of an artist she watched herself in mirrors, saw drawn features, the high and accented cheekbones of age, the ravages, not of time, but of loss; and she despised Jeremiah. She listened as hatred flared among us, hot hatred because people wanted someone to blame. As guesses turned to rumor, then to conviction, it became obvious that it was Jeremiah who dealt in flame. People cursed his name. Men sought for him throughout the valley, and swore vengeance.

Our destroyed world, what had it been? Abandoned farms, abandoned fishery, and dregs of memory that recalled honest lives and loves. Many of us had come to this place in search of spiritual amity, of community; but all of that died long before the fires.

"But," Debbie said to Mac on a gray morning before the bar opened, "how much of this sits on our own shoulders?"

Mac, who since the fires had remained largely silent, did not answer. Debbie turned from him and watched Sarah, because Sarah's shock seemed deepest, bone-breaking deep. Sarah made coffee and muttered Bible-text about king Nebuchadnezzar who God changed to a beast "...*that you shall be driven from among men, and your dwelling shall be with beasts of the field; you shall be made to eat grass like an ox, and you shall be wet with the dew of heaven....*" and then Sarah's voice whispered gabble, as though she spoke in tongues.

"The sumbitch rubbed our noses in our own lives." Mac moved like a tired man after a twelve-hour shift. Gray light crowded against windows of the bar in the same way that, beyond the burned church, cattle crowded fences. Mac picked up a broom, looked at it like he could not understand its use, then leaned it against the bar. He sat on a barstool and waited for coffee.

"...*and he was driven from among men, and did eat grass as oxen, and his body was wet with the dew of heaven, till his hairs were grown like eagles' feathers, and his nails like birds' claws....*" Sarah's voice trembled with fear or ecstasy, and Debbie could not say which.

"That preacher drove himself," Mac said to Sarah, as if they were holding a normal conversation, "and he's driving us right now because he was serious, and we only think we are." He turned back to Debbie. "He's not in the fields. He's ashes. He's across the road right now, ashes in his burned church. I watched him set the fire. I walked away. He didn't." Mac turned back to Sarah. "He's preaching right now, if you listen you can hear... what do you hear?...or, maybe it's the voice out of the whirlwind... like in the Book of Job."

It seemed to Debbie that, if Mac were not exhausted,

he would be nearly as hysteric as Sarah. "I hear nothing from across the road," she said, "and if he chose to burn it's his expiation, not ours." Even though she detested Jeremiah, her mind filled with sorrow. Then she felt guilty without knowing why. And then, she felt something she could not at first understand. She had not felt joy in many-a-year.

She began to understand a little. Her first understanding was that she no longer despised Jeremiah. She fell silent. Listening. It seemed to her that from the fields came a sense of movement, the herd movement of cattle; and from the coast, echoes of screams.

"You're right about one thing," she told Mac. "He rubbed our noses in our own lives. Even if he's ashes, he's still doing it because nobody's leaving town. We're all still standing here, and we're unreal. We're staring over fences."

"The dreams were real," Mac whispered. "We're the husks of dreams." He looked across the road where white-faced cattle stood in mist. At the intersection of roads trucks slowed. An engine roared as a tractor-trailer driver caught a higher gear. Another engine roared. "Why did the guy do his own atonement and leave us holding the bag?"

"That's a cop-out," Debbie told him. "Dream new dreams and quit blaming the other guy." Debbie paused, alive in the knowledge that Jeremiah had failed with Mac but had succeeded with her. Jeremiah had forced them to hate him, had sickened them, so that they must rebel against their lives or die. He had fought that they might once more learn to love. There were many arts, and many roads to them. Maybe Jeremiah had been traveling a road of art, and not religion.

Debbie yearned to comfort Mac and Sarah, and yet she knew that would be wrong. She felt, in some harsh way, ordained. She watched Mac and saw that her words were going nowhere. But, Mac, being Mac, would think about them, so maybe later... and then Debbie made her voice stern, nearly punishing, and hoped it would not break with compassion.

"The world is full of gurus," she told Sarah above the roar of truck engines. "Find another one. Lacking that, you may want to consider a question."

SCIENCE FICTION, UTOPIA, AND THE SPIRIT

Science fiction lies smack-dab on an intellectual center bounded on one end by teddy bears and on the other by youthful cynicism. It is often utopian, and in its pages battle the awful powers of good and evil. It is a literature of darkness and light (sometimes of sin) which carries sensibleness mixed with inanity. It is, more often than not, a morality play.

The genre could hardly be otherwise. The bulk of its readers are young, although many of its readers are exactly like its writers. The bulk of its writers are men and women who manage to retain their first childhoods well past the time when they might have slipped into their second. Science fiction, whether we are reader or writer, is the business of the child who remains within us. What is more, that child is an important person.

Let us remember our youth. At age seventeen the world seemed improbably mad. We were given moral codes, social codes, religious codes. Our bodies seemed awash in liquids, our minds a conflicting net of "thou-shalt-nots" and "I gotta's." If we were good children (as most are, though scampish) we were inflamed and confused by a world that tolerated every vice while howling after divinity. Some youngsters take a backseat and ride out the whirlwind. A few become crazed or suicidal. Some drop out. Others become compelled by ideas, because they need to figure out what is going on. One method of figuring has been immersion in science fiction.

Science fiction encourages such figuring because it allows its writers and readers to do what standard literature does not. Science fiction can deal with ideas as from a soapbox or a pulpit. For example, as a thirteen-year-old in 1945, I was reading science fiction that talked about racial discrimination, and about the horrors of holocaust long before they became polite subjects among polite people; or in mainstream literature. In those days the mainstream writers were either dancing on the issue, or writing nonfiction, or in the case of Sinclair Lewis: howling (Kingsblood Royal was one elegant howl.)

Only science fiction tried to analyze the ugliness. There were reasons. Briefly, standard literature tries to enlist our understanding by a complete showing of situation and character. It does not try to make an intellectual approach to understanding, as is often the case in science fiction. And, of course, tons of exceptions exist. There are mainstream books that preach, while quite a lot of science fiction attains to the state of mainstream literature. When the subject is religion, though, it is science fiction that steps forward; generally smelling of roses. The young, both writer and reader (and we who have retained our childhoods) move easily toward explanation. With religion, our approach is often made with a good deal of freight. I would like to take a look at a half dozen books which try to handle that freight. Such a look provides an overview.

The books are: *Brave New World*, Aldous Huxley; *After Many a Summer Dies the Swan*, Aldous Huxley; *Stranger in a Strange Land*, Robert Heinlein; *Past Master*, R. A. Lafferty; *Bug Jack Barron*, Norman Spinrad; and the greatest of the group *A Canticle For Liebowitz*, Walter Miller,

Jr. Aldous Huxley at first used the soapbox. He is best remembered for his *Brave New World*, which was his vision of Hell.

Brave New World has Henry Ford as its God, with perpetual amusement and consumption the only ends of society. Babies are conceived outside the womb and raised in factory production lines. Every material want is satisfied, including drugs (soma.) Under the slogan "Everybody belongs to everybody" sexual intercourse becomes routine. One only gets in trouble by settling on a single partner. Worship of Henry Ford exists in common conversation as "Our Ford." People are perpetually young for sixty years, then die to make room for new production. Since one consumes little while reading a book, the only cultivated senses are physical. Society lives in da da land.

At least one contemporary writer shows *Brave New World* as completely prophetic. In his critique of television culture, *Amusing Ourselves to Death*, Neil Postman demonstrates that we need not fear the approach of Huxley's hell because we're already in it.

When Huxley discarded the soapbox and ascended the pulpit he wrote *After Many a Summer Dies the Swan*. The book speaks of mortality, immortality, eternity; and praises death as solution to the problem of retrogression. In Huxley's scheme we grow downward to the animal state as we age. Too much loss, too many steaks, and too many worn ideas chip at our humanity. Fear and respect for civilization vanish.

The story begins in southern California with Huxley lighting satiric fireworks. An Englishman, Jeremy, of scholarly pretensions and no courage arrives to catalog the Hauberk Papers, purchased by the multimillionaire Jo Stoyte from the supposed estate of the raunchy Fifth Earl of Hauberk.

Multimillionaire Stoyte has no fears, except a fear of

death from which even his great wealth will not save him. He lives in a castle furnished with the finest religious art from Europe, a parody of William Randolph Hearst (but it could as easily be J. P. Morgan.) Stoyte's household includes his fluffbrained concubine Virginia, Dr. Obispo, his goatish physician, and Pete, a young scientist so innocent he believes Stoyte and Virginia are only friends.

Pete endures hopeless love for Virginia, and dies because of it. Meanwhile, Dr. Obispo is the one who makes out. At times when he is not seducing Virginia, the doctor works on problems of longevity. He studies the chemistry and life spans of fish. The scholar Jeremy will eventually discover that Obispo is on the right track. In the writings of the Fifth Earl, Jeremy finds that the key to immortality lies in eating carp guts. The story ends when the principal characters travel to England to see the Fifth Earl who is more than two hundred years old and still alive. It is a hideous ending.

It makes a good tale, but is interrupted by a character who lives in the neighborhood. William Propter is a scholar of religion. When Pete becomes confused, or Jeremy becomes bored, the reader encounters a conversation with Mr. Propter:

"And what is God? A being withdrawn from creatures, a free power, a pure working. His vigilance gradually ceased to be an act of will, a deliberate thrusting back of irrelevant personal thoughts and wishes and feelings. For little by little these thoughts and wishes and feelings had settled like a muddy sediment in a jar of water, and as they settled, his vigilance was free to transform itself into a kind of effortless unattached awareness, at once intense and still, alert and passive...."

Or

(Love) "The word's the same as the one we use when we talk about 'being in love'... Consequently we tend to think that the thing we're talking about must be more or less the same. We imagine in a vague, reverential way, that God is composed of a kind of immensely magnified yearning... Creating God in our own image. It flatters our vanity."

Mr. Propter's way is the way of the western mystic. Perhaps one-quarter of the story is given over to explanations and speculations. Such work does not serve the cause of literature, but it offers young readers some options. There truly exists a state of peace that passes all understanding. That may not be new news, but its actual existence is news for the young.

From a high and thoughtful attempt I turn to a work of intellectual tutti-frutti, and do so with sorrow. Robert Heinlein was a hero of my youth, and when I read *The Man Who Sold the Moon*, I wished to be exactly like him. His *Stranger in a Strange Land*, however, is only interesting for its succession of cheap shots. Heinlein, at the time he wrote *Stranger*, had become a political and social conservative. Thus, his book is not only shabby, it's an exercise in hypocrisy.

A spaceship filled with husband and wife scientists goes to Mars. There is some hanky-panky. A bastard child is born. He is raised by Martians after all members of the expedition kill each other, or otherwise die. A second expedition returns the young man to earth. Using Martian philosophy he will become a new Messiah, preaching "Thou Art God." The happy grasses are God, and presumably a cat is God. The kicker is that this is not animism, and is impossible to understand unless one can speak Martian. Unfortunately, the reader cannot speak Martian, nor could the author.

The main shepherd who steers the young man is an aging hack writer who has read a thousand religious texts and realized none. He despises theologians, then espouses a theology devoid of all content except unlimited sex, unlimited power, and no responsibility for anything: in-

cluding washing the dishes. It was a book deliberately
tailored for the so-called '60s Love Generation, and it
purports to give sound religious reasons for bed hop-
ping and destroying your enemies.

Destruction, it turns out, is harmless and nothing but
a joke. Guns, and people who carry guns, are simply
turned sideways in time. That makes them disappear.
When those people reappear they are found sitting among
clouds and cracking one-liners while talking about "The
Boss." It is a showy, but not a satiric, performance by
Heinlein whose ancient wise men consistently speak like
teeny-boppers (see his nine-hundred year old man in *Time
Enough for Love*.)

In addition to breaking my heart, and felling one of
my heroes, *Stranger in a Strange Land* gives easy answers
and refuses to address questions. In a world where all
men and women become "brothers," and religiously bed
each other, is there any possibility of privacy or contem-
plation? When power is absolute, does not power cor-
rupt? Does mystery and reverence for a lover depart after one has had five hundred lovers?

There are further offenses in the book, including eternal youth which no sensible person would want, but
which was a big sales point in the 1960s. It only remains
to note that Heinlein's version of heaven was Huxley's
version of hell.

It sometimes happens in science fiction that a good
writer is compelled by a story that is too large for the
genre. *Past Master* by R. A. Lafferty is a book to swear by
and at. In this book the planet Astrobe has succeeded
earth as first in the human pecking order. It enjoys a
perfect society where everyone is rich, or will be rich by
accepting the system. The planet is planned, programmed,
mechanized, logical. Evil exists, however, as do things
which are dreadful. Programmed killer beasts read
thoughts and feelings. People who question paradise are

rapidly removed from paradise. Rebellion spreads as people flee the system and establish the communities of Cathead and The Barrio. Conditions in these places approximate the bowels of England's industrial revolution. No one is well, no one can be happy, and ugly death is certain. Still, people choose such horror rather than live in the golden state of Astrobe. A further horror lies in the feral strips surrounding the communities. These strips are filled with devouring beasts.

The leaders of Astrobe seek a world president who can solve their problems. Their choice lies between a mechanical man (a programmed person) or searching through history and reviving a great leader of the people. They select Saint Thomas More, bringing him from the past just moments before he gets his head chopped off in 1535. More, the author of the satiric *Utopia* is called forth to lead Utopia.

This is a wonderful premise, but the genre contains traps into which *Past Master* falls. Science Fiction may use soapbox or pulpit, but when ideas are not being argued there has to be action and event. Young readers — and some not so young — will buy random action ahead of character development and meaning. The trap came about because the author picked one of the most complex characters in English history, a character who lived in one of the most tumultuous times. In order to fully realize the presence of Thomas More, *Past Master* would require a ton of backgrounding, thus slowing the story. It's a credit to Lafferty that the story almost comes off.

Unfortunately, a good idea gets crippled. It is filled with all sorts of action and extraterrestrial critters. Some are symbolic, some are not, and the game of figuring everything out gets to be not worth the candle.

The basic book, though, is worthy. It purports to be about the death of a world, the death of a man (humankind) and the Godly and instant rebirth of both. This is valuable intent, but real value comes from questions raised and brooded over.

Given paradise, what are the human objections? What hungering after God, and after individuality, walks people toward hell; for, in *Past Master*, Thomas More's religion and church survive in perverse and distorted forms among inhabitants of Cathead and Barrio. Thomas More does not much value church or religion, the leaders of Astrobe value them even less, yet the fundamental question of the book is: Are we better off to live in a heaven with no God, or have God although the divine plan may contain great measures of torment? I can't help but wonder how the seed of the book would have sprouted if the past had not yielded Thomas More, but Jonathan Edwards.

Some books further other books, and *Bug Jack Barron* by Norman Spinrad knits skeins from Huxley and Heinlein. Once more the subjects are immortality and power: especially important here because the book (published in 1969) addresses the "1960s generation." Youth then, as now, had a hard time grappling with the idea of death. Youth had not even begun its battles with ego, did not know such battles exist.

The book is told in shucking 1960s *Clockwork Orange* legspread hunchbutt brainblast jive. Jack Barron, together with his black buddy Lukas Greene, and his bed buddy Sara Westerfield are "Baby Bolshevik Galahads" from the streets of Berkeley, and from demonstrations in Montgomery and Selma. As the book opens everyone has passed the dreaded age of thirty. Jack Barron hosts a network TV show (a hundred million viewers,) Lukas Greene is Governor of Mississippi, and Sara Westerfield has retreated into silence in Greenwich Village because she believes Jack has sold out. Three power groups are in conflict: Democrats own the government, Republicans own money but cannot elect a president, and the

SJC (Social Justice Committee) owns the blues. The SJC represents the poor, the minorities, and political malcontents. It is headed by Lukas Greene.

Jack Barron's scam is a call-in show. People who have something bugging them call in and bug Jack Barron. Barron then vidphones senators or bureaucrats purporting to seek justice. "What bugs you bugs Jack Barron."

Focus for this stew of conflicting powers is the Foundation for Human Immortality, headed by Benedict Howards who is a demonic echo of Huxley's Jo Stoyte. The foundation has fifty billion dollars in assets. For fifty thousand dollars it will freeze a citizen at the time of death, then maintain the frozen corpse until research discovers how to resurrect the dead and give them eternal youth. In the course of the book, scientists actually discover how to stop the aging process, thus granting immortality.

By the end of the book Lukas Greene has settled for moral and political defeat, not yet knowing that he will be the nation's next President. Sara is dead. Ghastly immortality has been achieved by Benedict Howards and Jack Barron; an ending even more hideous than the end of Huxley's *After Many a Summer Dies the Swan.*

Bug Jack Barron is about a world where politics and show biz replace God — at one point Barron thinks carefully of Christ, and how Christ would have sold out the same as everyone else. The book is filled with violent realizations.

"There's your definition of politics, grown men playing kid game, hate-games, to get some simple kicks I get off Bug Jack Barron, living-color, man-up-front, self-image is all. And that's cool. But the real difference between show biz and politics is nothing but hate...."

Or

"They're people, dig, people is all, but, baby, they're junkies. All of 'em power-junkies. that's what power does

to you, a fucking monkey on your back — just like junk.
First shot's free, kiddies, but after that you've gotta go
out and cop more and more and more to feed the monkey...."

Bug Jack Barron is so filled with rage that even the
jive becomes tolerable.

Before turning to what may be science fiction's greatest book, it is well to mention two others that do not
actually belong in the science fiction/religion fold; but
which come close. *The Dispossessed* by Ursula LeGuin is
science fiction, but only abstractly connected to religion.
The Goddess Letters by Carol Orlock is an exercise in the
fantastical, but is not science fiction. It purports to be
an exchange of letters between Persephone and Demeter.
The religion involved is the Elusinian Mysteries.

Faith guides *A Canticle For Liebowitz* by Walter M.
Miller, Jr. It is unlikely that any other science fiction
novel has better served the cause of religion.

Faith not only guides *A Canticle For Liebowitz*, it ac-
companies the reader through three ages of destruction,
three dark ages, and three ages of renaissance.

The world destroys itself with nuclear weapons in
the 1960s. The book opens six hundred years later at the
abbey of the beatus Leibowitz. The abbey stands in the
Utah desert, surrounded by barbaric tribes and mutant
people called "The Pope's Children."

I.W. Leibowitz was a scientist working in "defense"
when the world was destroyed. After the bombs fell a
movement began. It was called The Simplification. All
educated people, and all books, became the targets of
the Simpleton mobs. The church offered sanctuary.
Leibowitz fled to the Cistercians. After many years he
became a priest. He received permission from New Rome
to found a religious order named after Albertus Magnus.
Its task was to preserve human history. Members of the
order were "bookleggers" and "memorizers." The

bookleggers smuggled written records into the Utah desert where the records were buried in kegs. The memorizers committed texts to rote memory, as the dark ages spread across the world. Leibowitz was hanged and burned while following the faith.

In 2560 a wanderer, a Jew, directs the novice Francis to an ancient bomb shelter which, among other things, contains a blueprint and some actual writing by Leibowitz: "Pound pastrami, can kraut, six bagels — bring home to Emma." This, and other writing, is sufficient documentation for canonization. Leibowitz is canonized. The abbey stands through centurites on a plain of darkness as monks continue to hand-copy manuscripts from decaying originals.

The second section of the book opens in 3174. There are rumors of war. Thon Taddeo is a scholar who must depend for his living on the barbarian ruler Hannegan. Taddeo comes to the abbey to review the records called The Memorabilia... "full of ancient words .... detached from minds that had died long ago. There was little of it that could be understood. Certain papers seemed as meaningless as a Breviary would seem to a shaman of the nomad tribes."

Taddeo's presence signals the beginning of a renaissance. The abbot quarrels with Taddeo about the responsibility of a scientist. Taddeo makes the traditional plea that he is not responsible for the use of knowledge, only for its discovery. A new technology begins with his investigations, and barbarian war sweeps the plains.

Meanwhile, the old wanderer, the Jew, has become a hermit in the hills beyond the abbey. After six hundred years he is still waiting. Outside the doorway of his hut he has a sign in Hebrew which he claims means "Tents Mended," but which is really Deuteronomy 6:6, "And these words which I command thee this day, shall be in thine heart."

The old Jew goes to see Thom Taddeo, then turns away in disappointment. "It's still not Him."

The third section opens in 3781. Advanced technology produces a new civilization complete with nuclear weapons and starships. There are rumors of war.

Through the centuries The Memorabilia has been kept intact. It is now on microfilm. In case of nuclear war the church has a plan *Quo Peregrinature* which will send The Memorabilia, along with a colony, to another star.

Sufficient numbers of priests and bishops will go along to perpetuate the church. The third section of the book is a cry of faith, also a cry of anguish.

"Listen, are we helpless? Are we doomed to do it again and again and again? Have we no choice but to play the Phoenix in an unending sequence of rise and fall? Assyria, Babylon, Egypt, Greece, Carthage, Rome, the Empires of Charlemagne and the Turk. Ground to dust and plowed with salt. Spain, France, Britain, America — burned into the oblivion of the centuries. And again. Are we doomed to it, Lord, chained to the pendulum of our own mad clockwork, helpless to halt its swing? This time, it will swing us clean to oblivion...."

The old Jew has ceased to be a hermit and has once more become a wanderer. He names himself Lazarus — a man raised by Christ, but not a Christian.

A mutant woman with two heads has only one head baptized. The other head does not seem alive. It is like a child in a coma. The woman has spent her lifetime trying to find a priest who will baptize this second head. She goes to the abbot. As the world dies, and as the abbot dies, from the woman comes a miracle of rebirth. As it happens the horizons light with explosions, and the starship departs.

Science fiction is a game for the young, who, when reading tales told from the soapbox will likely respond to power. Yet, power is only part of the religious equation. For the young, and for those of us who are not so young, another dimension appears when literature enters the genre. In *A Canticle For Liebowitz* we step easily beside the eternal power of God, only to be struck dumb by realization of the Glory.

HALLOWEEN 1942

I was ten years old in '42, and trapped in the German-Lutheran wilderness of small town Indiana. Halloween of that year still lives in memory because threats of Hell spouted from every pulpit, while true fires of Hell rose above coal and wood-burning chimneys; and a real ghost walked.

In October of '42 our town lay stunned as Hitler, having leveled Europe, marched on Russia. The Battle of Stalingrad thundered; blood-stained symbol of an adventure that would eventually cost a million, six hundred thousand lives. However, that many people, and more, were already dead before the Nazi thrust.

In that Indiana town, where lived many third and fourth generation Germans, our people wisely concentrated their fears and hatreds on Japan. The Rape of Nanking had worked its way into local thought. Bataan had fallen, and government censorship could not conceal the Bataan Death March. Nor could censors hide the battle of the Java Sea. Government news hawks made much of the Battle of the Coral Sea, but its turn-around-significance would not be understood for years. Jimmy Doolittle led a raid on Tokyo, lost men (of whom some were captured and executed as war criminals.) Attu and

Kiska in the Aleutians fell to Japan; and Japan took Correigidor.

Difficult memories, these. It is also difficult to separate feelings about WWII, from those of localized wars that have happened since. America would lose 33,529 of her people in Korea, above 60,000 in Vietnam; but in this war 406,000 were lost; and that in a nation of 100 million (today we are 267 million.)

In that small town, Halloween usually progressed with boring predictability. Kids went costumed, soaped windows, and youths sixteen years and up, tipped over outhouses (yes, many people still had outhouses.) Occasionally, while stealing pumpkins to smash on porches, a miscreant would run into a farmer who carried a shotgun filled with rock salt. The blast tore the salt to dust, and the dust bored beneath skin so that the unlucky target "scratched where it didn't itch" for weeks. But all of that, as I say, was "ordinarily".

On this Halloween there were sixteen-year-olds, but few eighteen-year-olds, and almost no twenties. Those not in the Army were in the Navy, or the Army Air Corps; and it is with the Air Corps, and a piano, and a witch, that this story begins:

My family's across-the-street-neighbor-lady lives in memory as The Widow, for her last name is lost. She was only a little dumpy, wore plain house dresses, and had become reclusive.

She had a son, Darrell, age eighteen, and a daughter, Janine. When he was alive, Darrell made model airplanes that really flew. During my growing-up, and because of the airplanes, he was one of my heroes. He went to war; an early casualty, his bomber blown to bits with no survivors.

To a ten-year-old, Janine seemed ancient, but I now know she could not have been more than twenty. Even in that small town, where — if anybody thought about art they felt threatened — it was known that Janine was a musical prodigy. On soft summer nights, with windows open, she would play ballads instead of classical exercises. Neighbors gathered on porches, watched lightning bugs, and listened to the best musical renditions that most of them would ever hear. After Darrell was killed there were no more ballads, and the music became subdued.

The witch was Mrs. Lydia Kale. She was, it was rumored, nothing but a fearful old country woman moved to town shortly after WWI; angry and bitter from a life spent in a places so small that people walked to church. No one knew why she came. No one cared.

To a ten-year-old she meant fright. Most people, I believe, remember at least one "mean lady" from their childhoods, but Mrs. Lydia Kale really was mean. She would grab a child, shake and mutter. She would even send curses when a kid passed on the sidewalk. She insulted preachers (no one else dared), and she intimidated adults.

She remains a crazed figure, dressed as dark as night wings. Her hair did not flow in the wind; nothing like that. Her hair was as white as her clothes were black, and her hair was worn in a tight knot at the back of her head. No one knew what she hated most.

These, then, were the players in that Halloween when, dressed in an old bed sheet and wearing a "funny face" (our name for mask) I embarked after a warning:

"Do not," my mother said, "go to any house with a gold star." She was adamant.

During that war, families with sons in the service hung small flags in their windows. A silver star on a blue field meant a man still serving. A gold star meant a man dead. Some houses had both kinds.

What does a ten-year-old know? More, I think, than I believed when I sat down to write this small tale. I remember stepping into a wind-blown, leaf-blown night — 7 p.m. but midnight dark — with dry leaves scurrying.

Something was wrong with the night. Other kids trotted past, laughing and whooping. Older kids hid in shadows, soaping windows, or suddenly appearing as they tried to scare each other. A normal Halloween, but something was wrong with the night.

I could not get in motion. I sat on a step at the side of the house feeling "wrong." An adult would say that he felt depressed, perhaps beleaguered. Children did not then know such words.

I finally understood that it was Darrell. He moved out there in the night, standing in his own yard amidst gusts of wind, flying airplanes. I could, but vaguely, see him. I could feel him. I could even feel the balsa wings fight the wind, rise, and rise higher.

And what the hell did I know about death? All I knew was that Darrell would not hurt me. But he was supposed to be gone. Lost, somewhere in the South Pacific.

There came music in the wind, but only gradually. Janine, when at that keyboard, found comfort beyond religion, beyond philosophy. The music began as light finger exercises and light runs, the kind of practice that lifts wings.

They were, brother and older sister, somehow together. I don't know, and never will, if Janine knew what was happening. I do know that for what seemed a long time I sat waiting. The planes rose into the wind, the rubber bands that drove them somehow never unwinding. They flew and flew. Music lifted them; and Darrell was no more than a moving shadow.

I hope Janine knew. I think Janine knew. Because of what happened.

There was music in the wind, a ghost in the wind,

and so who needed a witch? And besides, Mrs. Lydia Kale was a daytime witch who never stepped outdoors at night.

Her clothes were black. Only her white hair was a trace of her slow movement through the wind. It came to me that Mrs. Lydia Kale must be very, very old. Music, or Darrell, pulled her forward. Wind, only strong enough to scatter leaves, seemed to press her back. She had to walk a short block, and yet it took awhile.

Twenty-five years before, back in WWI, our nation had lost 116,000 sons. Tales of that war still covered the town. And, Mrs. Lydia Kale walked slow.

It was a night of shadows. On the darkened back porch, and facing the yard where Darrell flew his planes, The Widow appeared. She moved timidly. The Widow was but a dumpy form, a darker shadow among shadows. The music did not crescendo, but began to rise. Some sort of fury, or anger, or sorrow propelled the music; but Janine was already a master. She had it under control.

The shadows came together, but gradually. Mrs. Lydia Kale walked along the sidewalk, while in the yard the planes rose. I think she saw nothing. I think she wanted to see nothing. The Widow stepped from the back porch, moving slowly to the sidewalk. In that dark night the two forms came together. I could only see the white hair of Mrs. Lydia Kale. It seemed, to a child, that there was but one person out there, white-haired.

I do not know why Darrell appeared, and can't say exactly when he left. Mystery lived in the night, and the two women who seemed to have become only one woman, stood silent. From the house the music became, for a few moments, tender. That must be when Darrell left.

And then the music began to weep. It filtered through the night, through wind, and across the street to ten-year-old ears. The three women held the night, or pressed it back. The young woman wept above her keyboard, wept with her keyboard. The two older women simply held each other and wept.

ON WRITING THE GHOST STORY

Approach the Cathedral from the south and walk around it three times. On the third time, stop before the second gargoyle from the southwest corner. Spin around seven times very slowly while repeating 'aroint ye, aroint ye, aroint ye,' and your warts will disappear.

And, wouldn't you know, that ancient man followed instructions and his warts dried up. The happy results might have caused him to figure that time and expense going into cathedral construction was money well spent. He probably said as much to his neighbors. Word probably got back to the local priest, and the priest had to deal with it; just as we do, today.

The priest would have said, "Miracle," or at least, "Blessing." He would be quick to point out that it was Faith, or the presence of the cathedral that caused disappearing warts. It was not the gargoyle. Or, maybe he would have said something else. After all, it was a long time ago.

Today, we might say "coincidence," or "the placebo effect." We might say, "Quaint story, and isn't it wonderful how even the ancients could spread a certain amount of bull."

Having said that, we could dismiss the story and turn away. We could, in fact, make the same mistake that many have made since the rise of science and rationality in the 18th century. The mistake is best termed "denial of evidence." In its way, it is quite as serious as previous mistakes that denied all rationality and/or science. The universe, I fear, is rather more complicated than we might wish.

For that reason (complication) and because unseen matters sometimes compel me, I wish to spend a few moments giving a definition, and making distinctions. There are reasons to write what I call The Fantastic, and they have nothing to do with notoriety, fame, or money.

Definition: The Fantastic deals in those elements of human experience unexplainable by logic or reason. Such elements may exist within the human mind, or they may exist beyond it.

As we approach distinctions, let us first acknowledge that just because we name something doesn't mean we understand it. We generally understand bull, but not always, because it's an easy excuse for not thinking. We feel that we almost understand coincidence, but coincidence sometimes gets stretched to the breaking point. It gets just too blamed coincidental. If miracles occur, we understand either "faith" or "gee-whiz," and that's about it.

We haven't the foggiest notion about the placebo effect. Physicians know it exists, and physicians use it as standard medical doctrine, but they can't explain it. Nor can they define or explain death, although they can generally tell when it happens. They cannot define life, though science struggles mightily to create it; and, when successful, still won't be able to explain it: only how they made it come to pass. We give names to things, partly, it seems, so we can live comfortably beside matters beyond understanding.

At the same time, it would be the height of stupidity to deny the values of science and rationality. Science helps our understanding. Rationality helps. Logic helps. I stand amazed, sometimes, at the complexities that science reveals about the natural world, and about genetics, physics, astronomy. The trick is to understand that science and rationality are not geared to deal with every problem.

There's a problem of matters that exist "beyond all understanding," a religious phrase describing religious peace. If the phrase didn't go beyond religion, we could categorize it and feel comfortable. To our discomfort, though, "matters beyond all understanding" do not reduce to a single category. Some people have proclaimed this for a long time.

For example, back in the 19th century a social philosopher named Herbert Spencer claimed that we live with The Known, The Unknown, and the Unknowable. Spencer was often a pain-in-the-intellect. He was conceited beyond belief [1] but at least he acknowledged something that the 20th century, and now the 21st, seem to deny. Some things are unknowable, and we live with a little less comfort when we accept that notion.

On the other hand, I here aver that too much comfort is dangerous, anyway, and that is one reason why I explore and write The Fantastic. My other reason has to do with history, a subject to turn to, later.

I first propose my discomfort. I do not know why a secondary power station in San Jose holds, for me, a sense of evil and dread. It's not the invisible strength that comes from the transfer of electricity, because no other power station causes such sensations. I do not know why I feel surrounded by peace and enormous power when entering a Tlingit cemetery in Sitka. I do not know why the late night roads through mountains or beside rivers offer sights more slippery than hallucinations; because hallucinations are positive things. I don't know why the voice of a father or brother suddenly sounds from the inner part of my mind, and saves me from being hit by a drunken driver. And, intuition remains a mystery, though I use it successfully in writing and in other forms of living.

I do know that intuition can be trained. In other days when I drove truck long distance, my intuition rose to the task as thousands and thousands of miles piled up. There came a time when, while pulling up the back side of a hill, I knew that trouble lay ahead: a wreck, a cop car, a washed bridge, a tree in the road... and I didn't "think" it or "feel" it. I knew it. This, despite the absence of clues. There were no lights in the sky, no sounds, and nothing unusual about the road.

I also know of an invisible world that some folks try to explain. The explainers speak of parallel universes, or past lives, or spirits. Perhaps one or more of their notions is correct. Perhaps all three are a crock, because plenty of flummery surrounds these notions. Phony mystics sell cheap tricks to the gullible: séances, mysterious rappings on tables, or flying saucer rings in hayfields. There's no end to the clap-trap.

And yet... there is evidence, centuries of it. Things Unknowable go on in the universe, but they also go on in the human mind. When rationality is applied to that Something, rationality generally ends up sounding silly.

For example, some who have had a near-death experience report seeing a tunnel of light. The rational explanation for this is offered as: "Your endorphins were kicking in. No wonder you felt wonderful."

It's a questionable analysis, and probably silly. When a person is dying, there's no evolutionary survival-reason for endorphins. That is especially true if one is dying without pain. As explanation, the use of endorphins seems an assertion of faith about biological fact. It is no better than tripe purveyed by the average faith healer.

There are at least four fields of evidence that rise among humans: religious, observational, luck, and creativity. Perhaps one or more are connected, perhaps not.

The first body of evidence concerns the religious and miraculous: the appearance of apparitions, or guidance by an unseen hand. The centuries are filled with reports of healings (Lourdes a modern example), visions, Joan of Arc, Joseph Smith, Mary Baker Eddy; and among contemporaries, the reported appearance of the Virgin Mary at Medjugorje. Such appearances are generally accompanied by revelations.

Guidance by an unseen hand has been reported so often in the history of America, that is practically a rib in our body politic. Many, perhaps most, substantial reports come from Puritans and Quakers in the 17th century. We have records of ships blown so far off course that death from starvation was inevitable; yet a sign in the heavens, and a correcting wind saved them.

One must approach such evidence with skepticism, but also with an open mind. After all, we have records of such evidence (in the western world) for over two thousand years. The odds on all of it being meaningless are impossibly long. There's just too much of it. We can't explain it. Perhaps we can't understand it, but it is the height of folly to deny that it exists.

Further, it is just plain impotent to say that if evidence cannot be duplicated, and thus subject to scientific method, it does not constitute evidence. There's no scientific way to explain sources of religious revelation. Yet, religious revelation happens over and over in history.

The second body of evidence is generally dismissed as illusory, or coincidental, or fabrications by unsettled minds. It includes ghostly sightings, flying saucers, possession by the Devil (or something equally nasty) and communications from the dead.

The standard responses to such evidence is generally, "It's a damnable lie," or, "Oh, lordy, I believe." Very few responses say, "I wonder?" or, "Let's examine the evidence."

If we do, we find that it is almost always intensely

personal. While the first body of evidence is sometimes communal, this second sort is singular. Groups of people hardly ever see ghosts. Flying saucers, or lights in the sky, may be seen by large groups; but encounters with flying saucers are almost exclusively reported by individuals or couples. Possession by evil is generally one-on-one (although when we arrive at a discussion of creativity we'll see it happen to groups), and messages from the dead are exclusively reported by individuals. (Group séances may well be unrepresentative because of a long record of charlatanism.)

This second body of evidence can be subject to both psychological and physical examination. Some people are amazingly neurotic. Some are insane. Some are physically unbalanced. And for some, there seems no help. It is as if some genetic flaw, some "bad seed" compels them. Physicians can measure brain waves and chemical imbalances. Psychiatrists can exert their skills. Between medicine and psychiatry many are helped and some are healed.

If we set aside all evidence given by those who are emotionally or physically injured, we are still confronted by countless reports from people who are as sensible as salt. They are not famous liars. Some of them are beyond reproof or reproach. They are not lying, and have no record of hallucinations. For them, at least, something happened. They can't prove it. Yet, because of who they are, and because of their great numbers through the ages, their testimony constitutes valid evidence. I would, for example, no more argue with the mystical knowledge of some American Indians, than I would argue with the sun.

Good luck constitutes a third body of evidence. It sometimes happens beyond all statistical probability. It is with luck of gamblers that we see evidence of something "going on" that cannot be rationally explained. It is probably statistically impossible to make seventeen or eighteen successful passes with dice, yet it occasionally happens. I have seen three royal flushes in a night of poker. The winning hands were held by different people. No one in the game had sufficient skill to cheat, and the cards were not marked. And, we were playing for pennies, thus with no great motive to cheat. Three such hands in one night (with no wild cards) are statistically impossible. Gamblers speak of "lucky streaks," and "hot dice." One branch of psychology speaks of "extra sensory perception."[2]

Bad luck is practically impossible to demonstrate, but scarcely anyone over age twenty-five has not experienced a year in which a series of major bad things happened. I'm sure we've all heard someone speak to the effect, "I wouldn't live 1988 (or some other year) over again for all the money in the world."

A fourth body of evidence is creativity, and of all mysterious evidence, creativity is the kind most studied by thinkers and psychologists. The creative process has been examined and documented. It is so commonly demonstrated that it appears in college freshman textbooks. It is described almost perfectly, and not a soul who describes the process understands it.

Nor do artists, writers, theoreticians, physicists, architects, musicians, dancers, or actors. In general, the solitary artist; i.e. the writer or painter or sculptor, will report that "There are times when it's all coming together, like somebody or something runs the show." The writer will say, "Thus, I'm not writing, I'm typing. Later, I clean up the language, but when the story is coming, it comes from somewhere else." Painters tell us that their hand knows what to do, even when they don't. Sculptors the same. I doubt if there is a single worker in the solitary arts who will not make such a report.

Group creativity is something else. The creativity of groups has received small interest from thinkers and psychologists. They speak of "mob psychology," but rarely go beyond the mob. And yet, the idea has been around for a hundred and fifty years.

Back in the 19th century the French social thinker, August Compte, postulated the notion of The Group Mind. He tried to apply it to small groups and to nations. His ideas did not fly. He could not get his fellow thinkers, including Herbert Spencer, to buy into the idea. It would be wonderful if Compte were alive today, because his thought might now be valued.

I doubt if there is a theater group, a dance troupe, or a jazz band anywhere in this country that will not attest that at some point in a play or a performance, the group takes over. There isn't a symphonic musician anywhere, who will not tell you that at some point the entire symphony pulls into a single mind and expresses the statement of the composer, and the symphony.

With the positive creation of art and music, I have little to think about. It operates so commonly in my life, and in the lives of my friends, that it gets taken for granted. It is negative creation by groups that I find worth examination.

I first stumbled on this when reading depositions of the Salem Witch Trials. I did not come unprepared to the reading. The 17th century was so fascinating that I'd studied somewhat of its writing, society, and culture. I was not an able historian, but was an able student.

Revelations abounded. It became evident that through circumstances (some beyond its control) Salem had gotten itself tied in a Gordian knot it could not slice. It was surrounded by other religionists (mostly Quakers) who held ideas that Salem considered evil. It had Indian problems. It had a tax rate as high as any in American history. It was isolated by weather for at least five months a year. Social control was held by the preacher. The educational level was nowhere near as high as in Boston.

The town was filled with bickerings, some petty, some substantial. Any deviation from the accepted way of "doing things" constituted a terrible threat. As I have written elsewhere, Salem, when it self-destructed, did not explode. It imploded.

In consequence, Salem created hell, and the Devil walked the streets of Salem. One preacher couldn't have done it, although through history plenty of preachers have tried. One politician couldn't have done it, nor could one farmer; or one of anybody else. It took the mind of the entire town to create hell, because in the creation, dissent was at first, silent. It was not mob psychology in any sense that we understand. It was genuine creation.

Once the proposition of group creation is accepted, it's easy to find all through history. The Nazis, for example, could not have gone so far, and so fast, had not Hitler been of the maniac quality that would build the group mind. An American historical example can be drawn from the witch hunts of Senator Joe McCarthy during the 1950s. A mob mentality did develop. Beyond that mentality, though, was a creative quality that produced a spirit of evil. We, who are old enough to have experienced it, will attest that something awful overran the mind of the nation. National insanity only faltered after McCarthy became so extreme that he became ridiculous.

The four bodies of evidence are simply that: evidence. They are not proof. Such evidence causes discomfort, and a certain amount of discomfort makes some people want to think things through. A lot of those people are writers.

Having accepted the fact of an invisible world, the writer may rightly ask: Is it my cup of tea? What can I do with it? Is it worth my time? How do I get a handle on it? Isn't reality difficult enough, without messing around in surreality? Is there something constructive about fantastical writing? Is it a valid part of the human experience, or is it only amusement?

Writers always find individual answers, because the task is individual. Some answer questions by saying: "It's amusement, and easy to sell." Others answer, "There's something going on and I need to examine it, because it needs come to the reader's attention." Such writers are usually worrywarts, or at least have some kind of mental warts. Writers who deal with the Unknowable, and with the power of the Unknowable — be it in the universe or in the human mind — tend to swing between practicality and downright mysticism. It takes immense courage, or immense stupidity, to mess with metaphoric gargoyles.

Writers choose fantasy, or magic realism, or science fiction. Others deal in horror, or allegory (as for example, *Watership Down* with its lovely thinking rabbits). For my own part, I am more than a little fond of ghosts.

II

One of the finest ghost stories I have read in many years is Peter Beagle's *Tamsin*. It contains everything that lies within the realm of a ghost story: character, situation, suspense, evil vs. good, innocence, heroism, and history.

The beauty of a ghost story is that it's almost impossible to write one without resorting to history. After all, if you've got a ghost, that ghost has ordinarily come from time past. (There are ghosts of the future, as in *A Christmas Carol*.)

As a fiction writer I think of myself as a historian. My history is not the pulling-together of a massive number of details, and the objective reporting and analysis of facts. I don't have that kind of ability, though capable historians are among the people whom I most admire.

A story is a different kind of history. It gives a

feel of time(s), place(s), and event(s). The skilled writer can take us into a world we would never, otherwise, know. While there are many places I cannot take you, I can take you to a small ship on the North Atlantic, to a mist-ridden hollow in Kentucky or North Carolina, and to the Washington rain forest. I can take you along empty roads, or to the top of tall trees, or to the bays and snows of southeast Alaska; and I can tell you how things look and feel. What is more, in the process of taking you there, I discover feelings and sights and whole landscapes that even I did not consciously know existed.

Thus, when events in the story happen, they happen in the context of what I know and report, but also of what I discover. If I were indifferent, and reported a context I did not know (for example, flying a sail plane) the context would be no good. With a sour context, events in the story would have no meaning in the life of characters; and thus the story would have no meaning.

But, if I stick with what I know and one of my characters is a ghost, I can give the reader the feeling of what is, and what used to be; and I can do it at the same time.

I, and you, when you think about it, can tell whether the writer of a ghost story actually believes in ghosts. Most don't, and that is one reason why there are so many lousy ghost stories. If a writer doesn't believe in ghosts, then he or she will have a terrible time suspending disbelief. The story becomes an exercise in special effects, only.

Knowledge of ghosts is not something one acquires through simple faith. Or, if one does acquire it that way, then one is intellectually stuck before a campfire warming his frontside, while getting chilled along his spine by spooky stories. Simple faith, without reason for owning it, seems pretty adolescent.

Knowledge generally arrives through experience, reading, and observation. By observation, I mean more than simply looking at events or the world. Observation requires thought.

Here is a simple example: I used to teach at a small university that boasts a magnificent campus. Old and new buildings are surrounded by huge fir trees that tower over rooftops. It is easy to walk across campus and say things like, "Wow!" The trees offer greater meaning, though, if one knows that the university was a hundred years old in 1990.

The university is in Tacoma, Washington, and Tacoma was once a lumber town. During the 19th century forests were chopped like grass before a lawnmower. There was no clear-cutting, though, because there were no chainsaws. Unmarketable trees were left standing. These would have been trees younger than thirty years.

When land was cleared to build a college, marketable trees went. The young trees remained. After one hundred years, it was a fair guess that the giant trees on campus were, give-or-take, a hundred thirty years old.

I could look out my classroom windows and feel the presence of those old lumbermen. I could see their tools: the steam donkey (a yarder for moving logs), their two-man crosscut saws, their axes, their teams of horses or mules hauling logs to mills, or to a steam railway that ran to the harbor. I could imagine them working through summer heat or winter rain in this wet northwest.

I could do all this because reading combined with experience. As a student of history, my reading about the northwest prepared me for a one-hundred-year old scene. My work experience had once been in trees when I worked for a tree company in Arlington Massachusetts. (There was time when I claimed a Harvard education on the grounds that I had climbed every tree on the Harvard campus. It was a bit of a stretch. There are a zillion trees on the Harvard campus.)

With that background there was no problem understanding ghosts. In my mind those old lumbermen busied themselves around that campus every day, and students walked among them. Just because no one could see them didn't mean they weren't there.

"Lordy," you say, "I'm reading the words of a maniac."

It's a possibility. On the other hand, we may be onto something. Suppose that our usual ways of looking at time and history are flawed. We think that Monday comes ahead of Tuesday, and when Monday is over we won't see another Monday until next week. That seems a real limit on consciousness.

If we admit, though, that the past operates with great force in our Monday lives, as well as Tuesday, and the rest, maybe we can step beyond the limits. In some ways, at least, we may live a series of Mondays. At least we live according to ways that are laid down by the past, and not by a succession of days.

Virtually everything we know and do steps toward us from the past. Let us look at only a very few examples:

Family. We may, through thought and experience, eventually create original forms. No one starts that way. Almost everything we accept or reject about human relationships began as learning in some kind of family group, even if that group was an orphan's home.

We are raised by people (usually parents) who were raised by parents who were raised by parents, etc. If one's grandfather was a farmer, then his son will know things about farming even if the son lives in a city. He'll know them because his dad tells tales, and the family sometimes visits grandpa.

Let's say the city-son hates farms. The grandson will also have an attitude toward farms. He's either going to embrace cows in order to offend his dad, or else he'll think ill of milking-time because "that's what pop told me."

Law: Our entire system of laws derive from English law and philosophy that reach far back beyond the Magna Carta. And, the Magna Carta has roots all the way back to the Code of Hammarabi. Six thousand years, give or take.

Society: We boast a diverse society made up of many people with different customs. Virtually all of those customs step right out of the past. A few, such as watching too much television, are fairly recent.

Religion: People who take it seriously, be they Christian or Jew or Muslim, have to take the historical Moses seriously. People who do not give a snip for religion still live in a world that does, so even an atheist has roots in the doings of Moses.

Even superficial matters like dress have already been decided. Contemporary men and women generally own pants, not caftans. Styles come and go, but only a very small percentage of us own kilts. This has been so in the western world since the peasant frock, and the Roman toga, hit the rag pile some centuries back. In a very real way, the past is right here with us, hanging off of our suspenders.

Briefly put, at least ninety percent of the way we live our lives comes directly from the past. To me it follows, then, that just because I can't see things invisible, does not mean they aren't there. The creative eye learns to see them because the creative eye trains itself to look.

The challenge for the creative writer, and the creative reader, is the same as the challenge for painter and sculptor and musician. In order to dwell with ghosts, we need learn how to feel the joy and pain of the past. Otherwise, no spirit rises from the pages, or canvas, or stone. Compassion is wanting.

As this essay is being written, I'm reading *The Tide At Sunrise*, a history of the Russo/Japanese war at the beginning of the 20th century. If I had not read a lot, and been around quite a bit, the history would seem fairly objective and cold. Not a single ghost would be present.

But, I have read, and I have been around. I remember Pearl Harbor. I have read *Shogun* and *Sayonara* and *Fires on the Plain*. The overwhelming devotion of the Japanese to their emperor during the Russo/Japanese war does not surprise me, and I expect to find it where I do find it; in the joy of soldiers marching to certain death. I mourn those soldiers, but I also understand something of their joy.

And, I have read Karl Marx and *The Communist Manifesto*. I have read a history, *The Fall of the Great Powers* which, among other matters, tells of the arrogance and violence of Czars Nicholas I and Nicholas II. I have read the humorless Solzenitzen and the gentle Abram Tertz, both of whom did time in Soviet prison camps. I know the state of the Russian people as the 20th century opened. Thus, do I understand the dogged determination of Russian soldiers and sailors even though their situations were doomed. I can feel their fear, and how they longed for a home they knew they would never see again.

Spirits rise from the pages. I'm not dealing with dry fact, but with human hopes and fears and dreams. Does it seem strange to mourn Japanese soldiers now dead these hundred years? Or, does it seem strange to mourn the same for Russians who were so badly led, and so heartily defeated? If it did seem strange, I would have no right to be a writer, and no right at all to tell ghost stories.

But, if the writer and reader do understand that men marched to their deaths en masse, but died individually, then writer and reader are ready to understand the presence of ghosts.

Ghosts are, first of all, a metaphor for history. The metaphor becomes strong as the ghost becomes strong. When the ghost is an actual character, as in *Tamsin*, the past rises and mixes with the present. The reason so many good ghost stories cause uneasiness is not because they scare the reader (although some do), but because they take the reader into two dimensions at the same time.

It is this dual quality that causes a ghost story to succeed. For that reason, one can write a ghostly tale and not scare anyone. If a ghost is a metaphor, in addition to being a character, then the ghost is in the happy position of being able to help the living. We have a friendly ghost, and I don't mean Casper.

Let's look at it this way: The ghost is someone (or, as we'll soon see, something) manifesting a spectral life after death. The ghost became dead for any number of reasons, including its own screw-ups. If, for example, it died while trying to drive a fifty-mile-an-hour curve at eighty, and if it appears five hundred yards before that curve on late Saturday nights, there's not a message of threat, but one of salvation.

Equally, ghosts bearing messages need not be people. They need not even be animals. They can be mountains and cars and ships and trees. Creatures or objects of the past gain fantastic reality when they become ghosts in a ghost story.

I am absolutely sure, for example, that if one has

lived in the American Southeast, and not seen ghostly soldiers and horses moving silent through mist, than one has not been paying attention. I am positive that if one climbs a one-hundred-foot tree, and while resting, does not feel a presence; danger increases. It increases because the climber does not have enough respect for who he's with.

If climbing tall trees is too scary, try walking through an auto graveyard where wrecks have been sitting for so long that weeds grow through floorboards. Be there sun or mist, watch what's happening.

Thus can we understand that ghosts of people, and sometimes ghosts of machines, are there to help the living. If, for example, generals of WWI had turned back to study the Russo-Japanese war, and acknowledged the hundreds of thousands of men who died, those generals would not have then destroyed an entire generation of English and European men.

The generals may have read the casualty figures of the Russo-Japanese war. They may have nodded their heads with pretended wisdom when they thought of assault against mountainous or dug-in positions, or defense of those positions. They may have read the record.

What they didn't read were the spirits who rose from the record, and those spirits were twofold:

The combatants on both sides were going through the first war with truly modern weapons. Their ghosts would have explained that nothing anyone ever knew about war applied. Something different was happening. Something awful.

The other ghostly, and ghastly spirit would have been a weapon, a machine gun. Had it rattled its voice in the ears of WWI generals as they marched their troops to war, a half a million men might not have

died. But, then, generals do not believe in ghosts.
They did not learn from a ghost that a single weapon
had changed war forever.

Thus, are ghosts among us bringing messages. I
have discovered that they exist, more often than not,
to offer aid instead of fear. I have grown fond of
them because they have so much to teach.

---

1 In his old age he practiced what he called "Cerebral Hygiene"
which meant that he read no books except the ones he had written.
2 As a young man during the '50s I recall resistance to the whole
business of extra sensory perception. A favorite story of the
time, and one that was probably true, said that the President of
the American Psychological Association was on record: "If
there was a tenth this much evidence to prove something else, I
would believe it. If there was ten times the evidence to prove
this, I still wouldn't believe it."

THE GHOST OF DIVE BOMBER HILL

Dead men at the bottom,
A roller-coaster ride,
Smoke 'em if you got 'em,
then hang a right and glide,
with fifty thousand gross...
and slide....

Headed north from Knoxville, trucks crossed into Kentucky just above Jellico and below Corbin. The road ran two lane and thin. That was "back then." Today I-75 carries the load out of Tennessee to Louisville.

Bessie has passed into the mists of time, although she lies buried on a rise above Dive Bomber Hill. Her house used to stand where now lies her grave. Her girls have moved away.

But the ghost still wanders the Hill. These days tired farmers see him, or he's seen by highschool kids who get the kind of drunk that mostly happens in places where, each election, bootleggers and preachers get together and vote the county dry. The ghost now seems a little lost, and still beholden to the living. No matter how successful he was in life, he made some big mistakes as a ghost. These days he's got no visible use except to waken tired drivers, or sober up a bunch of fool kids who think they'll live forever; and end up dying in droves.

Dive Bomber Hill hasn't changed. It still runs two lane and thin. An occasional tractor-trailer still moves along Highway 25 between Corbin and Mount Vernon. The rig rolls beside narrow shoulders, deep ditches and sharp hillsides. Northbound, it labors like a red or yellow smudge through foresty hill country, green in summer, gold in fall, and stark in wet winters. The truck's stacks generally smoke from fouling injectors, and it puffs gray or black on upshifts. When the grade drops hard, the jake causes cracks like rifle shots. Hardwood trees are bright in autumn and creeks still run. The land is alive with deer, varmints and birds.

At the crest of Dive Bomber Hill the driver hangs a right and, whoops, over she goes.

It's a two-lane, mile-long drop with a two hundred-yard flat space in the middle. That long flat space once held Bessie's place, fair-sized restaurant white-washed, bunkhouse, and a graveled parking lot filled with tractor-trailers. Young trees grow there now.

Coming off the flat space, the road plummets to a short steel bridge that rattles like chattering teeth beneath the tandem. Through the windshield what appears is the shear side of a mountain, a rock face. The road hangs a 90° to the left and points up the next set of hills. What used to happen... don't try this at home... don't try it on Dive Bomber Hill, either.

Dry freight haulers, and only them because no other type of rig had the right suspension, would hold back a handful of rpms as they crossed that bridge heading at the rock face. Speed, 50 to 60. As they came to the hard left they jerked their wheel left, then right, then left, and goosed out the last thin line of power. The trailer picked up and actually walked across the road, dancing like a truck practicing ballet.

That meant the driver could find himself starting to climb the next hill at 45 or 50. If the curve was driven according to all rules of sanity, he would find himself hitting that grade at only 20. How fast you can approach a grade makes a big difference on a hilly run, especially when you've got a dispatcher who thinks of the world as flat lines on a road map.

A man had to be on his game. Drivers not on their game produced some of the most godawful wrecks and bloody corpses the road has ever seen. Unless, of course, the rig burned. Either way, the guy and truck were pancaked… the grim joke being, "Anyone want to buy a tall, thin Kenworth?"

Then, one night, the ghost showed up and there were no more wrecks. Drunks still ran off the road and tumbled down the mountain. Trucks still sometimes ended up in ditches, but that rock face never again took another truck. Could be, it just could be, that the ghost knew he was going to have to pay off a debt.

The ghost knew drivers and their feelings. He seemed to know us better than we knew ourselves. For instance, sometimes a man didn't know whether he was on his game or not. When that happened, and he rolled away from Bessie's, the driver looked for the ghost to appear; lanky, sad-looking and gray as mist. Gray but luminous. The ghost dressed country-style but knew trucking. Under mist or moonlight, he always looked the same; thin face below white hair, the face stern as a ticked-off preacher.

The ghost would do one of two things: he would roll his hand in circles, the old road signal for "road clear ahead so roll em." Or he would pat the air, palm downward, like he petted an invisible dog, the old road sign for "slow it down." When he did that we would take his warning and drive like pussycats.

We: Jimbo, Mick and Luke-the-Apostle. I'm Mick, Jimbo is a wop… a skinny little ginny with ravioli eyes… and Luke, a Christian, but couldn't seem to help it. He didn't drink, smoke, chase loose women (although some chased him), cuss, gamble or do anything interesting except be a lay preacher on Sundays. He was sort of off in his own cathedral-type world. Me? As the saying goes, kiss me, I'm Irish.

Our trucks were '47 White Mustangs, six years old, engine rebuild at half-a-million, but lean and beautiful. They packed five-over transmissions that would keep a guy working in the hills.   Men swore that the seat was nothing but a board and seat covers.   They were a tough truck, in tough territory, what with hills and hijackings; both of which happened.   And, it was a sure bet that unless the schedule was totally shot, on every run those trucks would, soon or late, be found parked at Bessie's....

She was in her early fifties and just beautiful.   Even the youngest cowboy who ever strutted slowed down and looked.   Bessie was a little plumpish, with little-bitty face wrinkles, and always wearing a spiffy house dress.   Mostly her dresses were flowery, sometimes plain and decorated with flower-pins.   Her three daughters took turns "doing" Bessie's silvery hair.   What made her beautiful, though, was how she made a man feel.   The minute you walked into her place you just naturally felt peaceful.   For one thing, you had to hand your gun to one of the girls. She hid it behind punchboards over the sink.

Get seated at the counter and knots in the shoulders relaxed, the back didn't ache so much because the kidneys weren't bouncing, and it was like sitting around a country kitchen with country people.   Guys talked civilized with no cussing.   I've actually seen guys sit and help snap green beans.   It's hard to say, even now, if we showed up because of Bessie's daughters or because Bessie's place felt like the home we wished we had.

The girls, so help me God, were named Molly and May and Mary, with Molly being dark-haired, blue-eyed, and cute, May also dark-haired and cutting a fine figure, but more-or-less modest.   Mary was quietly pretty.   She had the brains in the family; bright, strawberry blonde, and sometimes a smarty mouth.   The girls also dressed in clean and pressed housedresses, flower prints, and with their hair fixed like ready-for-church.   Without meaning to, they were more attractive, and a lot more sexy, than any of the hookers on each end of the Knoxville/Louisville run.

In the days before CB radios news along the road traveled by truck. If there was a race riot in Detroit, people in Alabama knew about it before radio reporters had time to digest the news. Plus, it wasn't only news. Truckers, some of them, are awful gossips. If a man didn't know better he'd swear that b.s. never existed before the invention of trucks.

We heard about trouble at Bessie's while pulled over in the truck stop just south of Indianapolis. August heat lay flat across cornfields. Asphalt in the parking lot bubbled. Steam rose from ditches.

We'd been rerouted to pick up loads. Rigs ranged along the ready-line; Mayflower Fords, Roadway (roadhog) Express kicking Internationals (known as Binders), a few bright Reos here and there, Jimmys, Diamond T's, an occasional Marmon-Harrington; all in road colors of red, orange, yellow.

"You're an honest man," Jimbo-the-Wop told another driver. "You wouldn't be flippin' bullshit?" Jimbo took it serious. He sat small, muscular, sniffin' suspicious with an Italian beak that had already been busted one time in a fight. His hands were calloused and scarred like everybody else.

"I was there," the driver said. "I saw it happen." The guy was short, built like a fireplug, and capable.

We sat before cups of coffee. The place in no way resembled Bessie's. Like most truck stops the counter was three-sided, with kitchen at back. Guys looked across at each other. The design allowed management to overwork its waitress while keeping the boys happy; more or less. It all depended on, was the coffee fresh? Did the waitress look like someone you might have dreamed of, once?

"Turned out there was this old guy at Bessie's, must-a been sitting off to himself. Seemed familiar when we finally saw him. Seemed kind of gray and quiet." The driver paused, like he just knew he was about to be accused of bullshit. "You guys ever see anything on that road? Night stuff?"

"Who doesn't?" Luke said. He talked soft in the hub bub of the restaurant. The jukebox sobbed away on Truck Gypsy Blues, "...chasin' that lonesome road...."

Everybody sees night stuff. Luke calls them visions, I call them hallucinations, and Jimbo calls them hangovers. Different stuff appears on the road, and not just ghosts. Luke sees angels, I see animals that aren't there, Jimbo sees barns in the middle of the road with doors opening to let him through.

"So," the driver said, "some guys claim they see a gray ghost tellin' them what to do."

"We've heard about it," I said, admitting nothing.

"Suppose there is a ghost," the driver said, "and suppose one night he walked up to Bessie's like any normal man. Does that sound right? That don't sound right."

From what the guy said, we learned that three plowboys from London, Kentucky had showed up midweek, the week before. They'd been drunk, passing out crap, busted a chair and propositioned the girls, treating them like whores. They left the minute Bessie phoned the sheriff.

"So everybody's sitting there," the driver said. "Minding our manners, mindin' our own business. This gray guy ain't at the counter. He's maybe off in one corner at a table. Then these three sodbusters who didn't learn nothin' show up again. They're drunk and drivin' a crapcrate '41 Buick.

"The very minute they come through the door, Bessie starts moving. She takes a broom like she's gonna sweep those boys right into an outhouse... one of the damn fools makes a mistake. Instead of running he raises his arm against the broom. Bessie gets kind of bumped, falls back against a wall."

"Who's in jail?" Jimbo was believing the story. He no longer had doubts.

"I assume that one or more is dead." Luke didn't look like an apostle, really. He looked like somebody who ought to be running a hardware store. Just a quiet, smart guy with thinning hair.

The south has a few things to answer for, but it also has good things going. Nobody hits a woman, or if they do they get dealt with. Sometimes, some sorry fool is stupid enough to hit a woman in the presence of real men. It was damn near a death sentence in older days, and maybe it's changed, but I wish it was the same way now.

"Nine, maybe ten guys on their feet right away," the driver said. "We chased those bastards to their junk car. Just as the driver got the engine started this gray guy shows up. I admit to bein' scared, somewhat." The driver's hand actually shook when he raised his coffee mug. The coffee slopped a little.

"This gray guy, outta nowhere, stands beside the car and there's this spic driver steps up beside him; Spaniard or Mex, or some such-a damn thing. The spic reaches through the open window. He grabs the driver's hair and jerks the head down against the door frame. Then he lays a knife, honest to god, longer than your wanger, across this hayseed's throat."

"Okay, so far." Jimbo liked it.

"And then," the driver claimed, "the damn Spaniard starts out preaching woe about killin' bulls and visitations and general horseshit."

"It wasn't," Luke said real quiet-like. "What you're saying sounds like Jeremiah. Jeremiah 50:27."

It always seemed strange, talking about the Kentucky

hills while surrounded by civilized Indiana, which is as flat as a political promise. In the busy truckstop rigs roared off the ready-line, and there were rattles of air tools from the shops. Guys in the restaurant slugged five-cent coffee from thick mugs while they told stories about themselves being heroes.

"... sounded like horseshit to me," the driver said. "And the spic kept it up. The other guys stood, the whole bunch of us, watching and listening for maybe ten minutes and not able to do squat. Ever' time the spic made a point in his sermon he'd bang the hayseed's head agin' the doorframe, 'til the bastard wasn't just scared but sober. Ended with talking about evil and upright and blood-thirsty...."

"Proverbs 29:10," Luke murmured. "Most likely."

"And then," the driver said, "he drew that knife light across that throat, just enough to bleed. And then he gave the guy's head one more bounce, and let go the hair. And that Buick got out of there, throwin' gravel all the way to Miss-i-friggin'-ssippi."

"And nobody dead." Jimbo sounded indignant.

"Not unless the hayseed bled to death, which I gotta doubt." The driver gulped his coffee. "Then the Spaniard says, 'Mother-of-God, what happened? Did that shit come out of my mouth? I don't talk that way.' The Spaniard wiped the knife on his pants leg and looked toward the gray guy, and the gray guy wasn't there. And the spic says, 'Damn farmer wasn't worth goin' to jail over. How come you guys didn't stop it?'."

The driver tossed a tip on the counter and stood. "Turnin' St. Looie." Then he paused. "The thing is, there was a bunch of guys there, and that meant a bunch of guns behind the punch boards. Nary a one of us thought to go get one." He shook his head like he couldn't believe the memory. "And we watched the Buick leave, and then looked around and the gray guy still wasn't there, and the spic was still sore at us." He started toward the doorway.

"Keep it between the fenceposts," I told him as he left.

......

The outfit we drove for tried to keep its trucks running in groups of three. Driving the hills of Kentucky and West Virginia was no joke back then. Trucks that got hijacked were generally whiskey or tobacco haulers, but dry freight or swinging beef was fair game. Our outfit figured that a lone truck was a target, but three together were safe. Nice idea on paper, but hard to make work on the road. On the turn-around headed south, we generally held pretty close together until Frankfort, Kentucky, where a long, long grade leads out of town. The truck stop on top of that hill not only had walls of the can painted gleamy white, it supplied crayons so guys could write graffiti; most of which was on the order of, "Goddamn my truck."

Jimbo always led, Luke second, me at the rear pretending to supervise. When we got into the hills our little convoy fell apart. The only way anybody ever caught up to Jimbo was if some farmer in a '41 Chevrolet got ahead of him, 40 downhill and 30 up. Lots of times, though, another trucker, well ahead of that slow farmer, could see a clear road. He would give a road sign. Jimbo would catch the farmer on a curve. Even some country boys would give you a road sign when they could see clear road and you couldn't.

I trusted the judgement of truckers, didn't trust the country boys. Jimbo took chances with the country boys. He figured if they misjudged, and he got caught looking at oncoming traffic, he could always whip his trailer to the right. He would run the screw-up off the road.

The sum of it was that Jimbo always sat at Bessie's, licking away on his second cup of coffee by the time Luke pulled in, and his third cup of coffee by the time I got there. Made no difference whether summer or winter, we'd all three have wet armpits from busting gears through the hills. And, we'd all three be as tense as a rabbit with a case of the hots.

The parking lot was long and narrow, and when I pulled in there wasn't a ready-line. A gasoline Binder hauling for North American sat toward the end of the lot. Shadows reached toward it, with an August sundown sitting atop the western hills. A flashy new Ford convertible sat behind the Binder. Jimbo's rig sat beside the Ford, engine rumbling. Hot diesels were hell to start. The drill back then was to lock the doors and leave 'em idling. Luke's rig sat behind Jimbo. I set my rig square behind Luke. When I climbed down I'm looking directly at the bunkhouse.

It looked abandoned, and was. After WWII trucking had changed. The country could run a war using mostly railroads, but peace caused a need for trucks like nobody had ever believed, and the trucks were getting snazzy. Sleeper cabs replaced bunkhouses.

This had once been a fair-sized bunkhouse, maybe six cots. Now it sat as white-washed as Bessie's place, but with dusty windows and a padlock on the door. Decaying sunlight shone onto, or into, the dust, and it seemed like there was movement inside. Couldn't be. Seemed to be. Couldn't be. I peered through a dusty window. Nothing. The place was zipped up tighter than the Pope's skivvies.

I crossed the lot to Bessie's and expected Jimbo to be shooting a bunch of bull, depending on which one of the daughters had the counter. With Molly or May, Jimbo was just full of it. He didn't try tales with Mary, because Mary could answer up faster than an alderman. When I got inside, though, and laid my .38 on the counter, Jimbo sat and stared into his coffee cup. The jukebox complained that there was more rain in the road than there was in the sky. Something was wrong. Something dark.

Mary had the counter. The North American driver sat next to Jimbo on one side, Luke on the other. The guy flogging the Ford sat two stools down. Nobody sat at tables, not even that shaded table over in the corner of the room. Or maybe not. There was a little touch of mist over there, like tobacco smoke had collected.

"You're of a marrying age," the North American guy said to Mary, "But are you of a marrying disposition?"

"I think of it not a little," she said, "and a man could do a world full of worse." She glanced toward Luke. Luke blushed. Out there in the parking lot Luke's truck sat registered for fifty-six thousand gross, a truck that could pull the top off a mountain. It was a truck that ran through every kind of weather and every kind of trouble. It was a truck that could only be touched by a full-grown man who was no fool. And, yet, Luke, who was surely full-grown, blushed. Okay. Something going on between them. Maybe Luke spent Saturday nights here, not Knoxville. More than a case of the hots. More like a case of the quivers.

The North American guy picked up. "In which case," he said, "I'm a mite too late." He stood, paid for pie and coffee. He didn't ask Mary for his gun which meant he didn't have one. Furniture guys didn't really need them.

"Keep the rubber side down," Jimbo told him. Jimbo still stared into his coffee cup. He didn't make a move until he heard the North American roar into life and pull away. The dark feeling still covered the room. Windows across the front of the building let in light, but the light seemed defeated.

"Something," Jimbo said, "somethin's going on. Somebody's trying to sandbag this poor dago." He looked toward the guy with the Ford convertible.

"Could be," the guy said, "that it's none of your gaddam bidness." The guy was one of those turning-to-fat heavyweights. He had piggy eyes, and tried to dress city. Checkered pants, narrow suspenders. He looked like a chubby pimp or a used car salesman.

"Could be," Luke said quietly, "that it's some of mine." Luke might look like a hardware store owner, but didn't sound like one. In the south you don't worry when a guy starts yelling. You worry when a voice goes quiet and calm.

"Could be," Mary told the local guy, "that one claim-jumping deputy is in over his frowzy head." To Luke, she said, "Take it easy." She turned and headed quick for the kitchen. When she came back she was followed by May who took the counter. May looked onto the parking lot. "Furniture haulers," she said about the North American guy. "Gypsies. You hardly ever see them twice." She sounded almost wistful.

"Bring your coffee," Mary told Luke. "We'll sit in your truck and talk."

I watched them walk outside, both shy as teenagers on a first date. Waves of heat rose from the road, but was nothing compared to the heat between them. Mary could not have been more than twenty-two and Luke maybe five years older. And both of them virgins, most likely. I wanted to tsk, thought better of it; wanted to laugh, thought better of it.

"Start any bullshit," May told Jimbo, "and I turn you into wop soup." She grinned as she said it. "You could, I reckon, spread just a little."

Jimbo turned to look out the windows. Luke and Mary were still walking to Luke's truck, but now they were holding hands. "What's she want with Luke? Preachers ain't no fun."

"He's smart," May said. "And she's smart. I got the

looks, she got the brains. She'll marry a preacher or a teacher, or something. I'll end up with somebody like you." She was right about the looks. May had hair nearly to her waist, but done up high. She had full lips, blue eyes, a smile that could soften rocks. Her figure was like in *Esquire* magazine, and her sass like Sophie Tucker.

The heavyweight stood up. Looked at May. Looked at me and Jimbo. Made a decision. "I'll be back," he said. "Tell your ma." He headed for the door.

"Coffee's on the house, you cheap bastard." May sounded just a little hysteric.

The guy turned, reached in his pocket for change, thought better of it when he looked at Jimbo, and left.

"Don't go nowhere," May told us. She reached behind the punchboards. "Keep 'em hid. Ma's got a rule and I'm breakin' it."

My .38 was a snub nose. Not hard to conceal.

"Don't go nowhere until another truck comes in. We got no man around this house. Not always." She looked toward the dark corner of the room. Looked through the window toward Luke's truck. "Our daddy was a preacher, and we miss him," she said about Mary. "I expect that's why she's attracted." She turned toward the kitchen. "Fatso is gone."

Movement in the kitchen. Molly showed up, little and cute like a colleen. Lots of Scots-Irish people in these hills. I kept watching the clock and wondered just how far off schedule this would take us.

"Get ma?" Molly sounded like she didn't know whether to be afraid, or get so mad she'd stomp her foot.

"Not now," May told her. "Bully-boys are cowards. He'll wait."

"We're losing minutes," I mentioned. "At least let us know what's up." Through the windows, where dusk already lay across the lot, I could see Luke and Mary walking back from the truck. They walked slow and somewhat pretty.

"We had some drunks run out of here," May told Jimbo while ignoring me. "One got a little bit cut and bleedy. He's the brother of a deputy. The fat boy is another brother, only in construction. He fills potholes for the state. Quite a family." She didn't say more because Luke and Mary came through the doorway.

"Brush your hair, missy," Molly told Mary. Molly couldn't be more than eighteen, but bossy. Mary looked rumpled, Luke looked flustered. Maybe a good bit had happened in that truck, but it was clear everybody kept their pants on.

Luke blushed, Jimbo chuckled, Molly fussed, May winked, Mary brushed, and I turned to the windows when I heard a downshift coming off the hill. A new Mack pulling propane eased onto the lot.

"Pete," May said about the propane driver. She turned to me. "Thanks, guys. Keep it out of the ditches."

Luke was whispering to Mary. "Get rollin'," I told him. We passed the propane driver on our way out.

I figured we were free and clear and not too far off schedule, but figured wrong. The ghost appeared at the top of the hill which surely meant something wasn't right. He'd never appeared all the way at top. This time he gave the road sign for "trouble ahead," the hi-sign; right hand stretched forward, palm out, fingers spread. We took him serious since there was a deputy in the neighborhood.

Sheriffs didn't bother truckers. Sheriffs were elected and needed friends. Truckers spent a lot of money in poor areas. Sheriffs didn't want to get a bad name for running away business.

State cops didn't bother truckers, unless the guy was weaving. They always allowed at least fifteen percent over the limit. State cops were trained.

It was deputies that caused trouble. They were usually young punks who worked cheap, because a red flasher and a badge made them feel like their ding-dong was longer.

This red flasher showed up right away. Sunlight had decayed to twilight, and shadows lay long across the road. The punk came wailing past me in a '50 Mercury, siren yelling high and thin against those forested hills. He pulled in between Luke and Jimbo.

Jimbo flipped his marker lights four or five times, which, knowing Jimbo, told me he was ready to start something; if I was. He eased to the shoulder which was none too wide. The deputy pulled in behind him. Luke pulled in behind the deputy.

I admit to some impatience. Instead of pulling in behind Luke, I stopped right in the roadway beside the Merc. The Merc sat boxed between three trucks, and three drivers who weren't expressin' a hell of a lot of charity.

I didn't even climb down. Just waited for the punk. He came around the front of Luke's rig, already losing his nerve. If he'd been in control he wouldn't yell. He looked to be late 20s, but already had bad teeth. His hat must be minus a sweat band because it was sopping. He had greasy hair hanging out below the hat, the hair all straggly around his ears. He vaguely resembled the Fatso guy who'd been flogging the new Ford. He started yelling at me to clear the roadway.

I spoke low and slow and pleasant enough. I told him that if I moved my rig it would be to push that frickin' Mercury off the berm and down the mountain.

His pistol was in his holster. He touched it, looked around, saw Jimbo out of his truck. The guy considered the odds, thought better of it.

"Stopped you 'cause there's construction," he muttered. "Road's busted up at the county line."

"Appreciate it," I told him. "Nice to know a man

who takes care of working guys." No sense pushing it.

He turned and stomped away. We pulled out, rolling Knoxville.

......

Pull the rig over, shut it down, let the warehouse guys have it, and sleep. It wasn't until day after, waking up for another Louisville turn, that we heard of a dead Fatso, though at first we couldn't be sure. All we were sure of was that August had turned to September, and there'd be more ground mist in the hills.

Jimbo and I sat in the ready-room with our rigs on the ready-line. We waited for Luke. Eleven at night. The road would be good for the first hour, get knotty in the second, and by two a.m. the drunks would all be off the road. The best hours are two to five when the only trouble is a deer or a razorback hog. Hogs are just short enough to get under the front axle, and tall enough to roll the truck. Rather hit a deer. Rather hit a bull. Rather not hit nothin'.

A driver came into the ready-room looking for coffee. His shirt was dark with sweat. His eyes were somewhat benzedrined but not too eggy. Just a tired guy after a long haul.

"Anything worth knowing?" Jimbo asked it, but either of us might. You could only get road information from other drivers. This guy looked like a thousand tired guys I've seen. He poured coffee and sat on a ratty couch with peeling imitation leather. The walls of the ready-room were institution-green, and his complexion about the same.

"One-a these days," he said, "I'm gonna buy a little store. I'm gonna sit on my sweet behind and sell all kinds of shit to truck drivers. I might even get married." He stretched, yawned. "Naw, that could maybe be pushing it." He licked away at the cup of coffee he surely didn't need. Habit.

"Helluva wreck," he said, "up by London. Ford ragtop tumbling down the mountain like Jacky and his girlfriend Jill."

"That Fatso guy?" Jimbo looked at me.

"Don't know who it was," the driver said. "Last I heard, they were still trying to figure a way of prying it off of him."

"One a week...." It was a road saying. It meant that if you drove for a living, you'd see at least one fatal accident every week. Cars were not well suspended. Roads were narrow, speed limits high.

"Woe betide." Jimbo couldn't help spreading b.s. He looked to the doorway where Luke had just entered. Luke looked like a guy who had been up half the night listening to a complaining wife. He wasn't bleary-eyed, but if it had been anybody except Luke I wouldn't have trusted him. He looked worn to a nub.

"If you wasn't drinkin' and smokin' and speakin' bad words and runnin' around with trollops...." Jimbo saw that flippin' it wasn't going to work. "What's happening?"

"I've been up to Bessie's," Luke said, real quiet. "I've got to get her out of there."

"Bessie?" Jimbo grinned.

"You know who."

"This is getting serious?" I pretended to take his news casual. "There's lots of girls in lots of truck stops."

"The Lord's work," Jimbo suggested. "Like predigested?"

"Maybe," Luke told him, "All I know is she's the right one. But there's a dead man now. Fatso's gone. You know what comes next."

...the Hatfields and the Coys. Feuds in the Kentucky hills lasted well into the 20th century... "You kick my dog, I shoot your dog, you shoot my cousin, I shoot your brother, you shoot my pa...." and on and on and on. Revenge. Dark. Deadly. Over in Bloody Breathitt county they'd shot a whole family, plus five sheriffs in six months, or six sheriffs in five months... I forget which.

"People are going to die, and all over fifteen bucks and stiff-necked pride." Luke poured half a cup of coffee and looked guilty for doing it. We were supposed to be rolling. "The drunk who got cut went to a doctor who charged fifteen dollars, so the cut must have amounted to something. The deputy tried to collect the money from Bessie. Then Fatso tried. Bessie told them to stick their gearshifts up their tailpipes...." Luke almost smiled. "Who would have ever thought that Bessie...." Then he sounded sad. "Now Fatso is dead...."

"Proves nothing," I said. "Let's roll."

"You know it," Luke told me, "and I know it. But tell it to the drunk. Tell it to that speed-trapping deputy. How many others in that family?"

"If you guys got any brains," the tired and bennied driver said, "you'll keep your sweet fannies t'hell out of it. Them hillbillies ain't responsible types." He stretched again. "...got a woman both ends of the line, but think I'll rent a room and try to sleep." He trudged away.

"Sin of pride," Luke muttered. "The deadliest of the seven deadlies."

The road in early September is generally clear. Trees are tired and ragged from summer, but leaves only droop. Few blow. In the hills the moon is often hazy because mist rolls off the tops of hills. The road can get hazy as well. Ground mist rises. Summer fogs turn the road into a mist-smoking path between trees. On downhills you let her roll, because you have to have something for that next grade. When it is late at night on smoking two-lane, trucking is better than best. Your senses are so sharp they actually cut the night. Falling down a hard grade at seventy, you have to be smarter than God, and twice as alert.

And it is on such nights that visions, apparitions, and ghosts appear. Giant moths flicker pure white as they drift high above the road, and an occasional night-flyer, dark and invisible, splats against the windshield. Headlights bore into the mist, and if a man is not a fool he slows. But, he doesn't slow much, because half of what he sees probably isn't there.

The ghost appeared at the top of Dive Bomber Hill, off to the right on the berm. I saw brake lights before I saw him. Jimbo's rig slowed, rolled past the ghost, and stopped. Luke's rig pulled in behind Jimbo. I pulled it over, climbed down.

Did I believe in ghosts? Hell no. Did I believe in this one? Hell, yes. Would I let my guys flail that turn at the bottom of the hill. Not a chance. Not with what had been goin' on.

The ghost wasn't doing anything. He's standing there like a luminescent glow against the black backdrop of the hills. He stood, just waiting, and he wasn't waiting for me, or Jimbo. We three walked up, and stood like stooges in a little circle before the ghost. Our rigs rumbled at our backs.

"The evening's entertainment...." Jimbo tried to flip it, but the words died in his mouth.

What we saw depended on who we were. Jimbo says he saw almost nothing but mist, at first. Then he saw a sidewalk preacher, the kind that used to come to town on Saturdays to bang their Bibles at street corners. I saw the figure of a man who raised his hand like a Cardinal, ready to sprinkle holy water while calling for money; pennies for the poor, dollars for the Pope.

Luke saw a father giving him a blessing. Luke saw a father's permission to marry a daughter. It could even be that a bit of scripture passed between them.

Then the ghost looked a little apologetic. Nobody could figure that out at the time. We climbed back up and coasted down to Bessie's. Five-thirty a.m., mist on the mountains, moon already down, dawn threatening. The only truck on the lot was a sixteen-foot van being flogged by a route driver. The sheriff's car stood near the doorway. One window of the restaurant was boarded up. Rock or bullet. Window gone. What with news about Fatso spreading up and down the road, and what with the sheriff's car, it was no wonder the parking lot sat deserted.

When we got inside the route guy was just leaving and it was family day at Bessie's. Bessie stood behind the counter looking cool as the morning dawn. She wore a plain housedress, light green and with a red flower pinned to it. Bessie was usually happy, but this time she was not smiling. The jukebox sat silent.

May, being the oldest of the girls, stood beside Bessie. Mary and Molly hovered down to one end of the counter. The sheriff sat real quiet and thoughtful. He was a perfect picture of a country sheriff, middle-aged, brown from the sun, muscular and capable. If he hadn't been a cop, he looked like somebody you'd like to know.

Finally, he said, "I'll handle Jerry, and tell him to handle Ellis." He sighed, like this was more trouble than it was worth. "A'course, Ellis and his sidekickers are drunks, and you can't ever be sure what a drunk is gonna do. 'Cause even the drunk don't know what he's gonna do."

"Arrest him," May said.

"And let him go," the sheriff said. "Just because we know he did it don't mean much. Best I can do is threaten him." He stood, rubbed his hand through his hair like he was trying to chase a thought. "I'll keep as close to it as I can."

"Tell those boys," Bessie said, "that's it's time to call it even. One cut, one window. I'll cough up the fifteen bucks, and let it go." Out there on the road a downshift cracked, a tanker slowed, then the guy must have seen the sheriff's car. He revved a shift and pushed it on down Dive Bomber Hill.

"… little late, and Ellis would have blown up even if you'd paid up, right off." The sheriff stood. "I can't tell you what to do, but it would be smart to hire a man to stay on the place… so Ellis don't make more mistakes." He looked kindly toward Bessie, and then left.

Luke watched him go, while Jimbo and I watched Bessie. Luke whispered something to Mary that I didn't catch. He had taken a seat nearest Mary, Jimbo beside him, and me beside Jimbo. Luke kind of scooched around in his seat. He put his hand on the counter. Mary touched his hand. I knew right then, that was the moment we lost him.

And so the deputy's name was Jerry, and the drunk's name was Ellis. It felt easier to hate their guts once they had names. Then I told myself that this would have happened, anyway. Luke was the kind of guy who, sooner or later, would leave the road. Truck gypsy blues. We've all had 'em. At one time or other we've all sworn we'd leave the road. Hardly anyone ever does. The road takes hold of a guy. But Luke… he might as well run a dinky restaurant… maybe better than running a hardware… he could keep up his lay preaching on weekends… maybe even get ordained… with a church… become respectable.

"A man?" Bessie said to her girls. "I never had but one man in my whole life, 'cause that was the only man I ever wanted. We'd not find anybody to come close to your pa."

"I have," Mary said. She kind of wiggled, which was sexy, but not what she meant. What she meant is that

Luke was a goner, and happy about it. She touched Luke's hand.

"A case of the hots ain't proof." May didn't believe it, even if May thought well of Luke. "You're talkin' about a truck driver, for hell's sake...." Then she shut up quick, because Bessie didn't allow cussing.

Bessie, real delicate, reached beneath the counter and pulled out this junky-looking 12-gauge double-barrel. She laid it longwise on the counter, the business end pointing away from everybody. I thought she was about to ask if Mary was in the family way. Then I thought nope, too delicate.

"You'll be wanting this," she said to Luke.

I tried to save him from himself. "We got a schedule."

"I'm quits." Luke said it quiet. "My place is here. I'll scout around and find a man to stay here until I can drop the rig. You guys go ahead."

"Leave it sit," I told him. "I'll bring another driver from the big city. You're done." I admit to being sore.

"Credit to you," Jimbo told Luke. "I never much held with preachers, but it's a credit to you." He didn't ask for his gun, because he hadn't checked it, what with the sheriff having been there. Jimbo looked almost sentimental. He turned to Mary. "You're a nice lady. My mom was a nice lady, and look what happened." He wrinkled his nose which had already been busted once. "Take a lesson, and good luck." He walked away.

"Could be," Bessie said real quiet, and still talking to her girls, "that your pa's still around here somewhere."

......

Maybe I didn't understand wanting a woman so bad you'd leave the road, but I did understand what Luke was thinking. In the south, in those days, a man was expected to defend his family with his life. If he had to kill somebody doing it, nobody complained. These days, if a man tries to rape your daughter, and you shoot him, you go to jail. If you're a bad shot and the rapist lives, he gets counseling... I'll tell a little story to show what I mean.

......

Back then, in one of the coal camps over in Knox county, a man got drunk and started beating his wife. She ran to her brother's cabin. Her drunk husband followed her and started banging on the door. Her brother yelled through the door. He said, "John, I know you're drunk, but I got a shotgun. If you come through that door I'll cut you in half. You know I got to do it."

The drunk came through the door. The brother cut him in half. The coroner's jury ruled that when that man came through that door, he committed suicide.

......

So I understood Luke, and I approved. It was just that it made a mess to have a truck stranded on Dive Bomber Hill. Jimbo and I rolled Louisville, phoned Knoxville, and Knoxville said "Leave it sit." They sent two guys in a car, one to pick up the truck.

Meanwhile, Jimbo and I got rerouted to Cincinnati, then back to Knoxville. A week had passed before we got back on Highway 25. By then we'd picked up a third guy, but the guy wasn't gonna work out.

His name was Sven, a hunky, and in spite of being Swede he had no Swedish steam. I put Jimbo in front, Sven in the middle in Luke's old place, and I batted clean-up. A couple miles before Bessie's we hit a delay.

The sheriff's car and the deputy's car sat on the berm, flashers twirling. A Chev station wagon, painted like an ambulance sat with its doors open. It looked like men were scrambling up and down the hill. Somebody off the road. Nothin' new. Happened all the time.

We got to Bessie's at four a.m. with morning still on the backside of the hill. The parking lot lay empty as a bootlegger's morals. Sven asked, "Why we stoppin'?" and I told him, because I wanted. We weren't even inside, yet, when a North Carolina rig pulled in, and behind it a Conoco tanker. Things seemed almost normal. Everybody headed in for coffee.

The busted window had been fixed. The place smelled like morning, the way truckstops smell when one shift goes off, another comes on, and the day starts over. Luke sat at a table in one corner. Mary had the counter. Somebody was moving around back in the kitchen. Luke looked tired as a man can be, like a guy who'd been crossing Kansas at forty miles an hour.

Jimbo and I sat beside him, and I waved Sven off. He went to the counter. Nobody said anything about checking guns.

"Keep this up," I told Luke, "and you lose weight in your behind. What's happening?"

"They won't leave us alone," he told me. "Like flies on honey. Like the plagues of Egypt. I run that Ellis guy out of here at least once a day. Plus his buddies." He looked through the windows. "See what

I mean?"

The deputy's car rolled onto the lot, rolled right up to the front door, and stopped.

"Move away," Luke told me and Jimbo. "I'll be needing room." He picked up that junky shotgun from where it lay at his feet. He didn't even stand, just laid it across the table pointed at the door. When the deputy came in he saw the shotgun, and stopped.

"Right barrel has birdshot," Luke said quietly. "It probably won't kill you but it'll hurt. Left barrel has a slug. It won't hurt much, because you'll be dead before you hit the floor. Which one you want?"

The jukebox started wailing about some babe wearing blue velvet. Mary came around the counter and unplugged it. The deputy stood in the doorway and watched three drivers at the counter turn toward him.

"Go away, Jerry," Luke said. "If you have law business here send the sheriff."

"If," Jerry said, "you are the sonovabitch who is running folks off the road, it'll take more than shotguns to save you." He turned away, and walked to his car.

"I want no part of this," the Conoco driver said. He stood, and Sven stood right along with him. They left.

The deputy's car pulled out slow and stopped before pulling onto the road. Something going on out there.

"Go see," I told Jimbo. He slid away.

"Tell me," I said to Mary, "'cause the gent with the gun is kind of groggy." I pointed at Luke.

"We're not married yet," she said, like it was the only thing on her mind. She looked at Luke. "He's gotta trust us to call him if stuff happens. He's gotta get some sleep." She looked through the windows, out toward the parked rigs. "Trouble. Better look. Somebody's about to go to Jesus."

I came out of my chair and was through the door before Luke could react. The deputy's Mercury had already pulled away, but somebody was out there. When I got to the rigs Jimbo had his .45 pointed right at a farmer. Ugly pistol. Sven stood looking like he was about to wring his hands. The farmer gasped, tried to talk, and was too scared. He was built blocky as a farm wagon, and looked just about as smart. An old Chev pickup sat beside the road.

"Cuttin' tires," Jimbo told me. He looked at Sven. "You'd better drive the east coast, pal. This road is too long and mean for you."

"Don't shoot him," I told Jimbo. "Not yet." The farmer whimpered. He looked like only his overalls were holding him up.

"One of Ellis' pals," Luke said. Luke arrived ten seconds behind me.

"I all the time ask the holy saints that I don't gotta use this," Jimbo said about the pistol. "Keep him covered." The farmer cowered. Jimbo moved quick, climbed in his cab, and came back with a tire billy. "School days," he said, "education time." He swung the billy against the farmer's left arm. We all heard the muffled crack as the bone shattered. The guy fell, rolled, and howled.

"You'll notice I picked the left arm," Jimbo said to Sven. "He can still shift gears. Take a lesson."

"How many tires?"

"Three."

I figured fast. If we took the spares from all three rigs we could make it, but good Lord, the delay. The only thing worse than changing a tire is mounting chains when it snows. I figured an hour lost, maybe more. No shop. No air wrenches... tire on wheel,

150 pounds... block up the jack... hydraulic jack with an eight-inch throw.

Take a chance rolling with cut tires? Not if I'm running the show. Not if anyone sane is running the show.

"Put the hayseed in his truck," I told Sven. "Get useful." To the hayseed I said, "Tell your boy Ellis he's done messing with this freight line. Next time the gun goes off."

The guy was hurting just awful, but you could tell he understood. Sven started his pickup for him, got him into it, and the guy weaved away headed for a doc. That's when Jimbo heated up.

He stood along the roadside looking up the hill where we'd seen the ghost. I can still remember it, plain as day. Dawn just back of the hill, the road running blackish-silver, drawing a line across the world, and Jimbo standing there like he was forty feet tall; despite he was short and skinny and tough. He shook his fist at the top of the hill, and he yelled: "You frowzy-headed jack-leg-preachin' old sonovabitch, you started this. If you're any kind of man at all, end it."

I thought he'd gone nuts. We got busy, working, and while I'm working I'm thinking. And this is what I thought.

If, back when Ellis and his boys first showed up, the ghost had not been so hot to deliver a sermon, none of this would have happened. The Spanish guy would not have banged Ellis' head against the door frame of the car, or laid a knife across his throat. It was obvious the ghost was the one who caused the Spaniard to do the ghost's preaching, because the Spaniard claimed it wasn't him. The sum of it was, I figured Jimbo was right.

And maybe somebody or something was running

cars off the road. It seemed pretty clear that the ghost might be well intended, but he had screwed up royal.

......

Our dispatcher got the story, and told me not to let the boys stop at Bessie's. He didn't have to tell me, but management generally figures that drivers are stupid. Even Jimmy Hoffa once said, "Any damn fool can drive a truck. I was a warehouseman."

We made another turn, then Sven took a job driving for Greyhound. I think what happened was Sven had finally driven Highway 25 in daytime and saw what he'd been driving through at night. It scared him right down to his gizzard.

The company assigned a Frenchy-Indian guy named Tommy, and Tommy was gonna work out. He could move slick as water running. Plus he had a sense of humor. "Women are just so trouble," he'd say, "'cause they all so cute and they so many of them. Wonder guys ever get anything done."

Which was good, that sense of humor, because otherwise the scene went dark. We didn't stop at Bessie's anymore, but I couldn't just forget Luke. In spite of being the marrying type, he was a friend. We'd put up a lot of miles together. What happened is, me and my guys would drop our rigs Friday evenings and not leave out again until ten p.m. Sunday. That's when the road is as good as it ever gets. That gave me Friday nights for sleep, Saturday for myself, and also Sunday morning. I flogged a one-ton Diamond T pickup in those days. It was a tough little truck, pretty as a race horse, lots of low end torque, okay in the hills. I drove to Bessie's.

When I parked beside the bunkhouse everything looked normal. A North Carolina straight-job with

an attic sat next a Mack pulling a lowboy. A D6 Cat
sat on the lowboy. An old Ford stake with hay racks,
a farm truck, sat in front of the Mack. Farmers
stopped at Bessie's sometimes, and that was all right.
Not all farmers were idiots. Just most.

When I got inside Luke looked lots better. At least
he'd had some sleep. Bessie had the counter and she
was jiving the farm guy about "he should come in
Tuesday," what with Tuesday being "wide-pie day,"
"slice 'n-a-half." The guy looked smart enough, and
didn't smell like pigs. The guy chuggin' the Mack
looked more like a mechanic than a truck driver. The
guy with the North Carolina job looked like he was
sick of hauling furniture. From the kitchen I could
hear Mary singing to herself.

"Outside," Luke said, "and I appreciate you're
here."

I followed him to the bunkhouse. The lock was
off the door. The place seemed roomy and had been
fixed up. Curtains at the window, a single bed and no
cots. A table and a couple chairs. "Staying here until
the wedding," he explained, and wasn't embarrassed.
"We're looking for a place."

Preachers. Go figure. The guy was determined
not to hop into the sack with Mary until after the
wedding. At the same time, he was ready to chop up
a deputy with a shotgun. Call me dumb, but somehow it contradicted.

"I don't actually believe this myself," Luke told
me, "except I have no choice. It seems that I have in-
law problems."

"Bessie?"

"Bessie is fine," Luke told me. "The girls are giddy
over the wedding. Big deal. Flower girls, long dresses,
the whole business. It's taking time." He pushed a
curtain aside and looked onto the parking lot. "Some-

place out there," he said, "my future father-in-law is a little too busy, and he won't listen. One reason he won't listen is because he's only about as solid as smoke."

I wanted to laugh. Instead, I shut up and opened my ears.

"That guy who got run off the road, the second guy, is one of Ellis' sidekicks. My problem is that he lived. He's in the hospital and the docs say he isn't crazy." Luke looked toward the top of Dive Bomber Hill. "The guy says that he braked too hard and spun off the hill because somebody was standing in the middle of the road. The guy says 'Ghost,' the docs say 'shook up,' and I say, 'Lord protect me from my friends.'" Luke sat on the edge of the bed and talked like talking to himself. "So we got one sidekicker in the hospital, one with a broken arm, and Fatso dead. That means I'm down to two, Jerry and Ellis."

"Those guys who are busted up are going to heal." It seemed to me like the answer was for Bessie and girls to get out of town.

"Not for awhile," Luke said, "and that boy in the hospital is a coward. Maybe a backshooter, but he can be handled." He sat, estimating. "The guy with the busted wing is blaming Jerry. Bad blood between them, so he's not a problem."

"The ghost?"

"...was Bessie's husband, the girl's daddy. He had a little church plus this restaurant. He tried to stop two hot heads from killing each other, and ended up shot."

"Might have stayed out of it?"

"He couldn't," Luke said. "The hot heads were in the parking lot, and his girls were in the restaurant. The girls were little more than kids at the time."

"Protecting his family."

"The problem is," Luke said, "he's still doing it." He stood up, walked to the window, walked back across the room like a man pacing a jail cell. "I don't know how this is going to end, but it will surely end badly."

......

It ended that same afternoon, except this kind of stuff never really ends. Makes no difference if it's between men or management or unions, or even nations; once bad stuff happens it keep bouncing like bullets off of armor plate. But, at least one ending came along toward evening. I wouldn't have known Ellis from Adam's off-ox, which was maybe a good thing. If I had known I might have prevented something.

Shadows lay real long across the road when I pulled away from Bessie's. Summer heat had faded and in another couple hours ground mist would rise. It would be a slow road because it was the time of year when crops come in. The road fills with flatbed farm trucks carrying side-stakes and hay racks. They are mostly held together with baling wire.

A guy almost feels sorry for the farmers. These are poor farms. If a hill farmer owns eighty acres, forty will go straight up, and forty straight down. There are places that are still farmed with mules because a tractor would fall off the side of the hill. It's said that men plant their corn with shotguns. Mostly, the farmers work narrow strips along bottoms and in hollows where streams always run.

And the farmers work hasty, like the devil is biting their heels, or at least they do in September. The last cut of hay comes in after the August thunderstorms. Farm crews work until daylight decays, then ride home in rattling hay trucks. The truck cabs hold three guys. If there are more than three men in the crew, they ride in back. You see them against a red sundown, tired silhouettes standing toward the front of the truck bed, holding onto the hay rack, and watching road. That's the kind of truck that was holding up progress when I got near the top of Dive Bomber Hill.

I found myself in a little caravan. The hay truck was in front, followed by a beat-up '41 Buick that looked as bald and ragged as its tires. I was behind the Buick.

Rust drew a line around the trunk of the Buick, and rust made the same kind of line around the back window. The junker blew a little smoke, but not much, and it bucked real hard when the guy braked, like a car about to kneel and pray. The driver tailgated up to the hay truck, swung out to see if he could pass, and cut back in. Cowboy stuff. Impatient to get somewhere unimportant. I might have known it was Ellis because Ellis was said to drive a junk Buick, but I wasn't really thinking. Just another slow down. There was a flat run two miles further on. Wait it out.

My pickup felt like a tin can, and, compared to an over-the-road rig, it was. It didn't stand high enough so a man could see much road. It was suspended like a brickbat on a roller skate. And, mind you, it was the best pickup made back then.

The sun stood just behind the hills. Trees, rocks, and cars looked like paper cutouts pasted against a red sky. A guy stood in the hay truck. He was also silhouetted, watching road. I hadn't noticed him before, but suddenly he was there. He steadied himself by holding onto the hay rack. He looked like just another farmer, or farm help, headed home at the end of a weary day. Then it came to me that he looked familiar. I almost hit the brakes.

Things happened fast, and yet it was like slow motion. It was like one of those movies where people get shot and take time flopping. The Buick gunned up to the rear of the hay truck, braked, fell back. An oncoming car flew past like the driver was late for an appointment at a cathouse; sixty, maybe seventy. And it was then that the guy standing in the hay truck, the familiar guy, turned and pointed to the Buick. He gave a road sign saying that he could see clear road. He rolled his hand.

The Buick jumped into the oncoming lane to pass the hay truck, and it jumped right into red lights twirling, because Jerry had been chasing a speeder.

Perfectly square, head-on wrecks, almost never happen. What mostly happens is two cars hit on the corners, and the backends rise and twist. Sometimes the cars roll. This head-on was only absolutely square one I've ever seen.

The impact caused Ellis' Buick and Jerry's Mercury to lift straight up, as much as a foot off the road. The sound was too sharp for a normal wreck. No tires squealing. Just explosion, while I ran the narrow shoulder to get the hell away from them.

The front ends of both cars disappeared, and the heads of both men appeared through windshields. Combined wreck speed, something in the neighborhood of 110 mph. Dirt and dust from the undersides of the cars burst above the dark road, and the cars for a moment looked like they rested on a cloud. They settled. The farm truck pulled over. I pulled ahead of the farm truck, because you don't pull in behind a wreck. You don't do it because the road is gonna get blocked.

There's no sense going into how it looked. The front ends were gone. The two heads, what were left of them, seemed to be trying to stare each other down. They did not look brotherly. I stood with a fire extinguisher expecting the worst, but the wrecks didn't burn. The farmer flogging the hay truck came up to me, took one look at the mess, and sicked in the ditch.

"You okay to go for a phone?" I asked.

He was all trembly, but no kid. "I can manage. What would make that damn fool try to pass."

"Because he's a damn fool." I wasn't admitting to nothing. "Go phone the sheriff," I told the farm guy. "I'll set out the flares." When he pulled away I took a moment to look at his truck. There was nobody in back, no man nor ghost, and the land was going darker.

......

I attended the wedding, and for a country wedding it was nice and not too corny. The flower girls were shirt-tail cousins from somewhere. Molly and May starred as bridesmaids, and Mary was prettier than angels. A country preacher, in a black suit that was slick with wear, and white shirt with frayed collar, managed to be dignified. Bessie looked sweet. Luke looked like a man who didn't know whether he was happy or trapped. I have no doubt that the ghost was in the neighborhood, but I didn't see him.

As it turned out, Luke was both happy and trapped. He worked with Bessie, and through the first few years Bessie's place prospered. There was no more trouble. Luke managed to get anointed, or ordained or whatever it took. He got a small church back in the hills and spent time both there and at Bessie's. He and Mary raised two kids, both kids bright and sassy. Time passes, though, and things change.

May married a banker in Corbin, and Molly went

off to Cincinnati. She got a job and went to college. She teaches in a country school. Bessie hired help for awhile but things were not the same. She retired and moved into London. Her restaurant stood empty until the fires.

Everybody guessed, but nobody could prove, that the fires came at the hand of one of Ellis' buddies. The restaurant burned, and Bessie's little house burned. Nothing to be done about it. At least nothing was.

Jimbo and Tommy and I ran highway 25 until the interstate opened. After that, I kind of lost track, except I saw Molly once in Cincinnati. She was just walking along a sidewalk, on her way to a summer class for teachers. We talked for a while. Bessie had passed on, and was buried on the hill where her house had been. Her girls didn't like it much, but they had honored her wishes.

And trucking changed. Lots of fancy rigs. CB radios happened, and that was one of the worst things ever. All of the comradeship came out of the road. There was nothing much left out there but bad mouths, bullshit, and cowboys turning the freeways into fester. Movies started showing truckers with monkeys and big-boobed babes in their cabs.

And, of course, we got old. Tommy went off somewhere, chasing a skirt. Jimbo actually married a nice Italian girl and settled down in Boston. I thought about such matters and decided against. The road had me, even after I retired.

It's a long road, and it winds and turns on itself. It goes somewhere, I suppose, but men who drive often only think they're going somewhere. I was in upstate Michigan near the Canadian border, and pushing a Dodge camper, when I thought of Dive Bomber Hill. Nothing much was happening in Michigan, so I drifted south.

Coming around at the top of Dive Bomber Hill, and hanging a right, the road looked the same. I rolled it easy and pulled off where Bessie's place used to sit. Nothing there but young trees and overgrowth. I slept for a while in the camper, and woke when the sun stood behind the hill and the sky was red. It seemed like the ghost had been waiting to meet me. Out there among the young trees a little pocket of mist moved as deliberate as a man pacing.

I waited. It didn't approach. I kept waiting. It moved up the hill. I waited until it was clear that the ghost wanted nothing much to do with me. It didn't dislike me, but it sure as hell didn't trust me. I waited until I finally understood that the ghost was doing the last thing a family man could do. It stood between the road and Bessie's grave, protecting the grave.

TRUCK GYPSY BLUES

I
Leave these blues behind me,
Let that tandem call,
Start that road to windin',
From it all.

Left a girl in Pittsburgh,
Cried to see me go,
Now these stacks are boomin',
Let 'em blow.

> Truck Gypsy Blues,
> Ain't no excuse,
> Make your own blues,
> Chasin' that lonely road.

Little Sue I love you,
Little Sue I tried,
But this road has got me,
deep inside.

II
Said I'll make just one round,
Then I'll rack my cue,
Said I'll take this rig down,
Just for you.

Then I got to St. Joe,
Caught a load bound west,
Said I'll pull just one more,
'Fore I rest.

> Truck Gypsy Blues,
> Love you refuse,
> Make your own blues,
> Chasin' that lonely road.

Little Sue I love you,
Little Sue don't cry,
Little Sue that road calls,
Say goodbye.

III
Well, I pulled from Pittsburgh
Pulled her in July,
Got back in November,
Want to die.

Found the house deserted,
With a note next door,
Said you'll never hurt me,
Anymore.

> Truck gypsy Blues,
> Cry your sad news,
> Made your own blues,
> Chasing that lonely road

Well the sleet's been fallin',
And it's ten below,
But that road is callin',
Gotta go.

WEIRD ROW

We drive the Reno strip before dawn and it's all bright lights and casinos: gin and tonic at 5 a.m., fancy ladies with drooping eyelids, the clank of old-fashioned slots and the zippity hum of electronics; an occasional rattle of coins. Dawn sees some gamblers weary with defeat and completely busted. They park before used car dealers and wait for the lots to open. They sell their cars cheap in order to get breakfast and bus fare home.

Me, and Pork, and Victoria (my comrades) drive through this glossy city as morning rises quick above the desert. We say very little, because Pork is dreamy and Victoria is crazed. We flee like refugees, though we don't flee far.

Storyland sits at city limits, between the town and the desert. When we approach, it looks like a hanger for monster airplanes, being of round metal roof and immense. It does not look like a book barn, though it is.

Once inside, Storyland stretches into distance like a stadium with fluorescent lights. Lights hang way, way up there, sending glowing messages from an awkward heaven. This is a freakin' church, a financial cathedral.

My comrades and I take our places before stainless tables, with dumpsters at our backs. I'm in the center with Pork on my left. Victoria giggles on my right. Dust collectors hum, conveyer belts slide slicky-sounding, and we snag packages from conveyors which trundle before us. We open packages. We work like dogs and are paid like dogs. Employee turnover is fantastic. Still, a few genuine nut-cases hang on; plus us. We like it here. We say we're on Weird Row. We're talkin' revolution.

The packages contain books, audios, videos, but mostly books. Thoughts and amusements of two thousand years trickle through our hands.

It works like this: The Corporation owns Storyland and sends books to every country in the world. Packages go out, but packages also come in. Packages arrive because when The Corporation receives orders it shops the Net. It finds needed books at small bookstores in Denver or Ashtabula or Cape Town. The small stores ship the books here for Storyland to resell. Workers who are higher paid repackage the books and send them to customers. Those workers get higher pay because what they do is boring. We, here on Weird Row, get the best part of the job.

Books on necromancy mix with Bibles, and children's picture-books rest beside dusty philosophies from two hundred years ago. History, evolution, how to raise a family cow... you name it, we open it.... all kinds and colors of books spit forth, plus: there is packaging.

"Plus," Pork reminds me, "there's Package Police." He checks the terrain with heavy-lidded gaze as he speaks. Conveyers hum all around, and other teams open packages. We don't speak to other teams. Who needs 'em?

Pork looks rested. Many years ago there was a song titled "Mr. Five by Five." That's Pork. Five foot tall and five foot around, like a giant bowling ball with a fluffy head. He has hazel eyes and the kind of beard you find on billy goats.

"There's also denouements." Victoria generally

sounds cultured. She is virginal and sweet and only slightly insane. She has no business in a candy-fanny town like Reno. Victoria should be gliding along marble halls while wearing a satin gown. She should be waving a wand that casts sparkles. Victoria is knock-down-dead gorgeous, little and cute, like a movie queen, like Hepburn. "There's visualizations," she says, "and actualizations and excitements. There's also a certain amount of stardust."

I make no big claim to sanity, either. If I am sane, why am I in Reno? My name…? it seems a guy would remember… I'm sure my mom recalls it, but she lives in New Hampshire. Around here they call me Smoke. Because I do, whenever I can sneak a butt. I'm skinny and going-on thirty with bright eyes and yellow teeth; a nice smile to go with it, a tidy little cough. I lust after Victoria. Fat chance. Lotsa luck, buddy.

"Package Police," Pork says, again. Even wide awake and rested, Pork sounds dreamy. Dreamy is dangerous. When he gets too dreamy, Pork fondles books.

The Corporation can't allow that. A man who fondles books is liable to steal something: a notion, an essence, an idea. A man who fondles books might learn a trade, develop a philosophy, found a religion. All through history, book fondlers have been known to commit creative acts. Around here, Book Fondling is a godawful sin.

After all, those books belong to The Corporation, and The Corporation has its own philosophy. The Corporation not only wants its fair share. The Corporation wants to own Everything. The Corporation will not be stolen from. Thus, the Package Police.

"Our plot marches forward," Victoria whispers. She is excited. She places a book titled *Teach Yourself Celtic in Your Spare Time* on the conveyer, then slowly turns to dispose of packaging. Recycle goes in one dumpster, reuseable packaging in another. The Celtic book had been wrapped in newspaper. A headline flatly states:

VAPORS EXCITE CAT SHOW
PULCHRITUDINOUS KITTY DEEDS FURBALL

"No story enclosed, just headline." Victoria speaks with some chagrin.

"None needed," Pork whispers. "We got enough to work with." Pork sounds as excited as Pork ever sounds, which is to say, real dreamy.

"Put a sock in it," I tell them. "We got problems."

A Package-Police cruiser has just pulled a U-ey at the end of our conveyor row. It heads toward us. The cruiser is electric and only big enough to hold one cop and one prisoner.

"Pulchritudinous," Pork says, and says it real dreamy. I give him a good nudge. He sort of wakes up.

This cop has missed his place in history. He's a perfect model for a Storm Trooper or an Alabama Deputy; an Adolph or a Bubba. He chaws on a toothpick and wears short sleeves to show his biceps. His brush cut stands spikey above blue eyes that can't help looking at the front of Victoria's shirt.

"You creeps, again," he says, and gives me a shove just hard enough to mess up what I'm doing. "Keep workin'."

I place a book titled *Ergonomics and Policy Reform in 13th Century Mesopotamia* on the conveyor. The packaging was bubble wrap. I toss it into the reusable material dumpster. Pick up another package.

This particular cop always shoves me when he's after Pork... something, Victoria always explains, that they teach you in cop school.

"You moved your lips funny," the cop says to Pork. "Say it again."

"Cheeseburgersforlunch," Pork tells the cop. It's one of our ready-made words. We have ready-mades for occasions like this. "We were talkin' lunch," Pork says.

"Before that we were talkin' breakfast."

"And now you're talkin' bull." The cop knows full well he's in the presence of subversion. He knows we're stealing thoughts, but doesn't have enough to hang us.

We got rights. The cop doesn't even have enough on us to justify a mild beating. He's one frustrated jock-strap.

"With French Fries," Victoria says, and says it most sweetly. She zips open a package containing *Pachyderms Of The Circus: Their Wit and Wisdom*. This one is wrapped in newspaper. She deftly, and with no seeming regret, tosses the paper into recycle. We who know her, though, feel her sorrow. We caught a fleeting headline, something like:

SYMPHONY GOES O AND 1 AGAINST
MENDELSSOHN.

Something to think about. And we will. As soon as we get rid of Adolph.

"We'd ask you to join us for lunch," I say in a loud whisper, "but then we'd be fraternizing." I figure the cop is so dumb he'll think it's a compliment. I think rightly.

"Another suck-up," he says. When he finally leaves we shelve Mendelssohn for the moment, then once more discuss a question of law.

It is true we steal words and thoughts, but we're not stealing them from the books. We're taking them from the packaging. Plus, things fall out of books: pressed flowers, locks of hair, clippings, (usually obituaries or marriages) bookmarks, snapshots, postage stamps, love letters, receipts, and postcards. It's all throw-away stuff.

So, if it's junk, who owns it? The Corporation says, "Throw it away."

"You can't steal something that's been thrown away," Pork always explains. "That's our fall-back position. When we finally get caught, and finally heal up from the beating, and find ourselves in front of a judge, that's our defense."

"Pulchritudinous," Victoria murmurs. "Nobody is gonna throw something like that away. That'll be their claim."

"Plus," I say, "they got lawyers. They own the judge. We got minimum wage."

"And the joy of combat," Pork tells me. "We got the pleasure of taking stuff right under The Corporation's drippy little nose." Pork can talk vicious when he wants.

"Every day," Victoria murmurs, "I take an idea, or an image, or a word away from here. I set it loose in the world. That, I believe, is Pulchritudinous." Victoria sometimes gets a dazed look whilst talking philosophy.

She is describing our mission. Our mission is not to defy The Corporation, but to subvert. We are warriors. That's the truth.

When books go out of here, headed for Bangkok or Plymouth-in-England, or Carrolton, Kentucky, they look just great. The Corporation has slicked them. Spots on covers have been cleaned. Torn dustjackets have been repaired. Lots of them look new, and all of them look snazzy. Like Reno.

But, I've seen inside some of those books. The words are still there, the ideas, the theories, the stories; but somehow life is gone. It's like everything in them is written on a dying desert wind. The books show color but have no heat of impassioned brains or beat of loving hearts. It's a giant gyp. The Corporation keeps the life of the book and sells the husk. Just like Reno.

Our subversion comes because we hijack words, ideas, dream-stuff, and yeh, occasional stardust. We hijack entire concepts, plus screwball visions. We can take a headline, a cat show, and talk it through. Then, we take it outside of Storyland and set it free. If our new idea or vision can make it beyond the city limits, it has a strong chance for a healthy life.

"Lunch," Pork says, and really means it.

We get take-out burgers at a roadhouse, then roll the car a mile into desert. The land is flat and covered with sage. In some places small hills rise, also sage-covered. We choose our spot with great care because The Corporation has spies. If we get caught, doing what we're about to do, the least that will happen is fractures.

I smoke a butt, smoke another. In the distance Reno seems to dance through heat waves, a tired and faded dance. The Corporation fits right into Reno. The Corporation came here because of tax stuff and central shipping. Birds of a feather.

We chaw on burgers, pretending that we hold a conversation about nothin'. We look here, there, every place. When we spot no spies, Victoria murmurs a little chant, tosses in a small but mystical spell. Then Victoria moves her delicate hand as if she waves a wand. She opens her hand. Pulchritudinous flies free.

Pulchritudinous dances like a tiny blue flame beneath desert sun. It rises above desert sage, skimming like a splendid little bird. It bounces playful. It dives, circles, and sports around us as it seeks a destination. It finally heads out in the general direction of Tennessee. It's gonna have one whale of a hard time making it in Nashville, but at least it's free of Reno.

"What is the difference?" Pork murmurs, "between Storyland and The Strip." He's talking, of course, about the Reno Strip.

"Us," Victoria says quietly.

I know what she means. Of course, Victoria is crazy, even if she does have smart brains. I search across the desert, but nothing out there moves. It looks like we've pulled off a successful stunt, but a day will come when someone spots us. Scary thought, but I don't think that any beating we get, or even any jail sentence, will allow The Corporation to reclaim Pulchritudinous.

"Time to get back to Wierd Row," I tell my comrades. "We still got to deal with Mendelssohn."

DADDY DEAREST

It began in a tearoom in Seattle, one with rose-colored table cloths and stained-glass lamps. A tearoom, I ask you. A tearoom with pictures of bunnies and duckies quilted on the napkins, the whole show run by a granny-lady named Mrs. Perkins.

In addition to bunnies the tearoom sported furniture like riff-raff from an antique store, you know the kind; a late Victorian breakfront, 19th century reproductions of 17th century chairs, and kitschy washboards, trivets, and unwarranted junk from rural America of seventy years past.

Into this tearoom, on one of those rainy northwest days specifically designed for funerals, slipped two quiet people who murmured to each other while touching hands. One, the man, carried a jar. The man (who looked like someone named Harold but who was actually named Aubrey) seemed nondescript in spite of grooming. His slender frame stood topped by brown hair, and he gazed about with brown eyes, a man eminently suited to brown; a man, one assumed, accustomed to brown thoughts, and it looked like he'd been thinking them for about thirty years. He dressed not in brown, but elegant tan cashmere and wool, most expensive.

The woman, smashingly beautiful, tended to the green of springtime. If the man seemed sad, the woman seemed only mildly serious. A touch of girlishness chased away rain and wind and gloom of streets where cars ran wet and umbrellas turned inside out. Whereas the man looked like a shirt advertisement, albeit a depressed one, the woman looked like an artist, which in fact, was the case. A bit bohemian, perhaps, but an artist who knew her business. Her piled hair looked Norwegian, her features classic Greek. She stood taller than Aubrey, not so elegantly dressed, but a green wool skirt fell just far enough to display trim ankles, and her green wool jacket snugged tidily around narrow shoulders. Name of Patsy.

The jar was one of those funerary things crematoriums give the bereaved, and which hold ashes. This cream-colored jar carried a gold leaf inscription reading: "Blessed is he who don't dip his finger into this jug-a-trouble 'cause he'll sure-God get it bit."

"I wanted a really nice inscription," the man murmured sadly. "Something from the Bible. But, Pop had to be snotty 'til the end. The whole memorial ceremony was compromised."

"It's been your problem all your life," the jar said. "Making compromises. Cutting deals where you come out on the short end of the stick. I tried to pay attention when you was growin'." The voice spilled from beneath the lid of the jar, no more than a whisper, but steady as wind across Montana. Aubrey looked at the jar, looked mournful, but not a bit surprised. He looked like he had been expecting something like this all along.

"Being dead doesn't seem to shut him up." Patsy suppressed a giggle.

"I had many a doxie in my day," the jar whispered proudly, "but nobody prettier than you." The jar chuckled, its voice not a little horny.

"I wish I'd known him better," Patsy said. "He's the

sort of rascal who seduces entire convents."

"He had that reputation," Aubrey admitted in a brownish voice. He held a chair for Patsy, then seated himself. "This is a nice place," he hissed to the jar. "Just this one time try not to embarrass me."

"I thought the memorial was actually very nice." Patsy looked around the room, at prints of kitties, piggies, and sunny children. She wrinkled her nose.

"My father's friends," said Aubrey, "were various."

"Apple knockers," the jar whispered, "and lonesome cowboys, railroad station agents, bar girls, torch singers, lady truck drivers, plus bozos, battleaxes... I'm talking here about ex-wives... lumberjacks, used car sales-men...."

"She gets the picture," Aubrey muttered. He also looked around the tearoom, looking at nicely dressed women at lunch. The women chatted about dreams and plans of husbands, sons, grandsons, daughters, nieces; chatted of piano lessons, while making distressed noises about Democrats and orthodontists. A few women cast cautious glances at the jar. They pretended nonchalance. The jar chuckled, the chuckle lascivious.

"I suppose one never gets completely away from his father," Patsy said. "But yours is a special case." She glanced through a menu. Her hair held just a touch of russet. She smiled generously and reached to touch Aubrey's wrist. "I'm not sure why or what you need...."

"For openers," Aubrey said quietly, "what do I do with him? I can't park him on the mantel at home. He'll just hit on the cleaning lady. I can't dump him. He'll turn into dust, and the dust will have a million teeney-weeney little voices. I'll be surrounded."

"We'll think of something," Patsy said, her voice a trifle cool. "You should look at your menu."

"There was a time when I dreamed you and I would become much closer." Aubrey blushed while Patsy brightened. He started to speak, blushed a deeper red, then waffled. "I feel uneasy with decisions unless we've talked."

The jar expressed a disgusted sniff. Patsy smiled. The owner of the tearoom, Mrs. Perkins, arrived to take orders. She hovered above the table like a beneficent deity of doilies, a lacy, gray-haired lady capable of expressing cupcakes with the wave of a hand, capable of cookies.

"Sadie," the jar whispered mournfully in the direction of Mrs. Perkins. "You must-of sold the brothel. You and the girls must-of retired." The jar sounded appalled. Then it began to hum, the hum sounding suspiciously like "Long Ago and Far Away."

"Did someone say something?" Mrs. Perkins sounded puzzled. "Is someone humming?" She gave a grandmotherly chirp. "At my age one gets to hearing things."

"...got a birthmark on her right leg, well above the knee...."

"Excuse me." Aubrey stood, removed his jacket, and placed it over the jar.

"Cucumber sandwiches, Darjeeling tea, and a pair of your lovely lady fingers," Patsy told Mrs. Perkins. Patsy smiled happily at the thought of lady fingers, certainly not at the thought of cucumbers.

"That one's gonna cost." A muffled whisper came from beneath the jacket. "I'll keep you up nights singing, 'cause I ain't sleeping, I'm only dead."

"A period of mourning is appropriate," Aubrey said after Mrs. Perkins left. "I can even get leave from the office. One does not lose a father lightly, even that father." He pointed to the lump beneath the jacket. His eyes shone a little misty, a man with more to say, a man about to stutter. Then he sat quietly.

"I'm not at all sure you've lost him." Patsy could not

suppress a chuckle. "When you stop to think of the power of fathers, and how they live in your life and your dreams, I'm not sure any of them are truly lost." She sat quietly, perhaps remembering her own father; or perhaps wondering when Aubrey would get to the point, if there was a point. "In your case," she said, "I'm sure you've not lost him. Have you wondered why this is happening?"

"Solar flares?" Aubrey asked. "Radiant energy from the center of the earth? Spaceships? Malicious gods? Time warps, bad luck, karma... do you believe in karma?" He reached to touch her hand, his touch tentative. "At first I hoped it a simple case of madness. Hearing things, you understand? I hoped it an aberration of grief. But, you're hearing him as well."

"And so is Mrs. Perkins." Patsy giggled. "You may be crazy. I may be crazy. But I double-guarantee you that a sweet old bat like Mrs. Perkins is not crazy."

"It's an out of body experience," the jar whispered from beneath the jacket. "I kid you not."

Tea arrived ahead of the sandwiches. Patsy poured two cups, raised hers in a toast. "To fathers."

"To fathers and to lonely nights," Aubrey replied. Another blush began, although his first blush had not yet finished. "Was there ever a chance for us?" Beyond the windows, in the gray light of autumn, traffic reflected in the polished surface of a store's large front window. Images passed back and forth as people mirrored in the glass. A teenage boy wearing a red baseball cap strolled past, hands in pockets and with a faraway look. He did not whistle. A policeman waited at a traffic light while three other people jaywalked.

"I love autumn," Patsy told him. "The world is just a little gusty before it goes to sleep for winter." She smiled, but her hand trembled slightly as she rearranged a napkin. "There still *is* a chance for us. Still is, but with alterations."

Aubrey stared brownly into his teacup as if reading leaves or searching for ultimate wisdom. "You're talking about my melancholy."

"You can do better," the jar advised Patsy. "With a bod like yours a girl could get to Vegas."

Patsy stood, took off her jacket, and piled it on top of Aubrey's jacket. Whispers of indignation barely sounded through the folds of cloth.

And it is true, without the jacket, Patsy displayed a delicate combination of features which would turn the head of any statue, if the statue were male. She touched her shirt front, realized she drew attention to some assets, blushed... then leaned back in her chair as cucumber sandwiches arrived.

Mrs. Perkins glanced at the pile of jackets as she set plates on the table. "We can't allow pets." Her mouth formed an unhappy line. "You cannot believe the strictness of the health department. If you have a little one there, he'll have to wait outside."

"It's not a pet nor ever was," Patsy assured her. "It's not alive." Patsy looked beyond the window and into the day of rain and wet leaves. She smiled at Mrs. Perkins. "A lovely day."

"I count myself lucky," Mrs. Perkins murmured. "So many friends have gone before me, yet here I am healthy and cozy in my little shoppe." Her voice trembled. "One does miss friends, though. Rather badly, in fact."

Unintelligible whispers rose from beneath the pile of jackets as Mrs. Perkins returned to her kitchen.

"Melancholy," Aubrey said. "It's all around us."

"A brown study," Patsy told him. "That's what old-time poets would have said. You're always in a brown study. Your mind must look like a piece of English tweed." Her voice, though critical, sounded tender. "My dear, dear man, with one life to live why must you choose only gloom and sorrow?"

Aubrey mutely pointed to the pile of jackets. He seemed near tears. Even his tan cashmere sweater appeared affected.

"Because a girl can't live with gloom," Patsy told him. "At least this girl can't. I'm basically a happy person."

"I think an evil jinn causes this." Aubrey pointed to the pile of jackets. "When I was child that..." his finger shook as it pointed "...that man denied my childhood. He made me clean out a chicken house. Worst day of my life."

"A chicken house?"

"Among other indignities." Aubrey sighed, but did not sound particularly sad.

"I'm looking at you in disbelief," Patsy told him, "because I don't believe a word of this." She stood, carefully removed jackets from the jar, and hung them over the backs of chairs. To Aubrey she said, "It's the restroom for you, my man. Get in there for at least ten minutes." Her tones were those with which one did not trifle.

Aubrey, bewildered, passed toward the restroom and beyond hearing. Patsy turned to the jar, her voice changing to tones most raspy. "Crap me around one time," she said, "and we head for the ladies' can. A royal flush will be dealt. Only one of us will return."

"Even if you can't do better, you can do different." The jar's whisper sounded impressed.

"I can't do either," she told the jar. "Even if I can, I don't want to. Artists are surrounded by people with weird egos. You can guess how a quiet and attractive guy...." She shrugged. "So, explain love? Go ahead."

"I have the time," the jar whispered sadly, "but you don't. You still have some livin' to do."

"What's this chicken house business?"

"The whole family had chores during a time when we went broke farmin'. He's not feeling sorry for himself, he's protecting his mama's good name. She pretended we weren't broke. Put on a few airs." The jar paused, the pause thoughtful, or almost. "He's his daddy's boy. He's got a sense of humor. He just never learned how to laugh."

"When he returns," Patsy said, her voice grim as graves, "I'll head for the can. You have ten minutes. Teach him to laugh."

"You two kids are gonna get along just fine," the jar murmured. "You are soundin' exactly like his momma."

"Ten minutes. He's on his way back here right now." Patsy grabbed her purse and left.

"One advantage in bein' dead is bein' able to tell the future," the jar whispered to Aubrey, after Aubrey returned looking unsettled. "…. Or rather, futures, because everybody's got a lot of them, depending on their choices."

"Give it a rest, Pop." Aubrey stood, looking like a man who did not know whether to stay or flee. He looked a little lost, and plenty lonesome.

"So I'm gonna tell you about a boy who could be you, a good boy 'til he married the wrong woman. He may hook up with the right one later on, or maybe not."

Aubrey sat, elbows on table, looking into the wet street. He pretended not to listen. He pretended he did not feel befuddled.

"This boy's daddy was a famous buffalo-rider of the old school," the whisper continued. "Won loving cups and stuff. When the buffalo-rider's wife had a little kid, he named the kid Spike; only the wife didn't like it and named him after some artsy-fartsy guy who moped a lot and died young. The kid grew and turned into the boy who married the wrong woman."

"Spike?" whispered Aubrey, and he seemed interested. His mouth twitched in a way that said it would be hanged if it was going to smile. "All my life you flipped b.s.

Aren't you ever ashamed?"

"Did I ever lie?"

Aubrey considered, looked at wet streets, wet leaves, slicky sidewalks. "... told some pretty wild stories."

"Every one true," the jar whispered. "This boy I'm tellin' about married this gal... she sold his furniture... rearranged his place... bought a goldfish named Clarence and a hamster named Rasputin. She donated his suits, all brown and tan, to a home for delinquent Arabs, and she decked him out in stuff that would get him shot in Milwaukee. He had to grow a mustache. The mustache shed down his shirtfront. Hair worked under his belt and tickled his crotch... caused a case of the hots... he goes home in a hurry... she's not home... he takes his case of the hots to a cowboy bar. Boy gets a snootful, ends up with a bargirl famous for card tricks, sharpshooting, bareback riding, and occasional hustles... they run off... live... you're chuckling, what'n'the hell's so funny?"

"You're trying to con me out of something. What?" Aubrey tried to make his voice brownish, and only managed something close to dark ivory.

"I got it on the line here, boy. Listen up, 'cause this is what happens with the second choice."

"Boy still marries the wrong girl. Boy still goes home with the hots. Goldfish intact... hamster happy... girl is home, copulation certain. Lots of hollering, rolling around, and in nine months out pops a kid. Name of Aloysius. Boy secretly names him Studs. Goddammit boy, there's a third choice, quit giggling...."

"Can't help it," Aubrey said. "You're running a con, and I'm seeing through it, and for once your b.s. isn't... hush, here comes Mrs. Perkins."

"Is everything all right?" Mrs. Perkins sounded the way a woman might, if a young man sat in her teashop talking to himself.

"Sadie," the jar whispered loudly as it could. "Long

time...."

Mrs. Perkins stopped, paused, looked around her tea-room. She checked out tea-drinking ladies, pictures of duckies, doilies, and lace. She quickly took a seat. "One of the boys from better days," she whispered to Aubrey, and looked fondly at the jar. "... give you fifty bucks for him...."

"He's my father."

"Forty bucks," Mrs. Perkins said. "I thought he might be someone else."

"Don't let her shove you around," the jar whispered. "A dozen times I've seen her run that number. You can easy get a hundred."

Aubrey laughed, practically helpless. Patsy, returning from the ladies' can, heard the laugh. Aubrey tried not to laugh, messed up royal, and laughed some more. Patsy took his arm, smiled happily, murmured something unintelligible, and Aubrey blushed. In the street, watched over by gods and flying saucers, by radiant energy and plain-dumb-luck, rain paused as if pondering a spot of sunshine; a new beginning, a blessed dawn. Then rain seemed to shrug its shoulders, puffed a gust or two, and decided to drizzle.

"I'm staying here with Sadie," the jar said to Aubrey. "You'll know where to find me." To Mrs. Perkins the jar said, "It's you and me, kid. You gonna display me on that sorry breakfront?"

"On my nightstand." Mrs. Perkins whispered so low Aubrey could not hear. Of course, by then, Aubrey had already helped Patsy with her coat and the two were nearly to the doorway, doubtless headed toward intimacy.

"On your nightstand?" the jar whispered, a whisper between awe and mild excitement. "You always was creative."

"We'll figure something out," Mrs. Perkins said, her voice throaty and bright as she watched Aubrey and Patsy step into the wet street. Aubrey raised an umbrella. He looked ready to tsk.

"I expect they'll be all right," Mrs. Perkins said. "But it's just going to be Hail Columbia for the first few years."

"It surely ain't a match made in heaven, plus he had another option. He could of learned to be a buffalo rider."

"It's a match made in a teashop," Mrs. Perkins said. "You'd be surprised how often it happens these days... no, nope, you wouldn't be surprised."

"I tried to be a good daddy," the jar whispered. "Take it easy, Spike."

"You have to cut them loose sometime," Mrs. Perkins said. "Let them make their own mistakes."

"She's too pushy," the jar whispered, "and he's a natural worrywart. A'course they're both good kids."

And Mrs. Perkins and the jar stood looking onto the busy street, a street of sales and traffic where it may be that a beneficent eye hovers godlike in the sky, directing the affairs of men, the affairs of women, and of women and men who have affairs; and then Mrs. Perkins picked up the jar and stashed it beside her umbrella where it would be handy when she closed shop and went home. She heard a slight sound as she turned to attend to customers, but missed seeing the jar nearly tip from the shelf as it gave a small hop and a jiggle, while weeping only a little.

JACKET COPY

"The superbly romantic novel of a man and three women... of intertwined loves and loyalties... of passion rekindled in middle age... and a dazzling exploration of hidden human depths...."

"Wow," I said, "exactly what I need." I was feeling extremely human and depth-ful at the time. I felt that my passions were due for a good rekindling. When your hair turns vanilla, and your bald spot increases, it seems you have to use more matches.

So I bought the book. It is titled *Daniel Martin*. It was written by John Fowles whose mildly spectral *The Black Tower* proved him one of the best writers currently operating in English. I preened and honed my passions. I checked my hormone count and hoped it would do. By heaven, I even rummaged around for a well-chawed old pipe, whilst donning a smoking jacket.

Daniel Martin is a fine book. Maybe it will stumble around through the annals of literature and finally be adjudged a great book. I have no quarrel with *Daniel Martin* except for some superficial treatment of a character named Jennie toward the end of the book. I am even glad to say that it is not a breathless book. The rekindled passions are curiously missing. What passions exist depend largely on Daniel Martin's revulsion of the modern world and his place in it. There are some English-y, squire-type passions as well, but it is best if we leave those to the Brits.

Still, that jacket copy sets a guy to thinking. If New York publishing was all that wrong, would New York publishing still be in business? I thought and thought, and did not like the answer.

But two can play the game. I decided that I would write copy for books that are faltering on the bestseller lists. It is the least I can do in the cause of literature:

Republican National Platform: "A Sizzling statement of Power... The Romance of Big Oil... Dares the reader...."

Democratic National Platform: "A Sizzling Statement of Power... Passionate... Intense... X-rated...."

The Congressional Record: "A Thriller... Finest mystery writing since Philo Vance... Greed rekindled in middle age... Taboo sex... taboo education... taboo intelligence...taboo Taboo TaBooooo...."

State Driver's Manual: "Not a book for the timid... Soft Shoulders... Curves... Blind entries... A sizzling manual of red hot instruction that has aided thousands... Thrill to the daring truth of lane swapping, and the frenzy of torrid youth learn to cry 'I Am'...."

Peterson's Guide to the Western Birds: "The faster you go, the faster you can go... Daring as a Marsh Hawk... Gentle as a dove... Raw fecundity with no fear of flying...."

Encyclopedia Britannica: "Brooding... Ghastly... Science gone mad... History amok... Evils of the human psyche, and the growl and sigh of Lost, Lost Worlds...."

Webster's Dictionary: "Revolutionary... Profound... Foregoing traditional devices of plot and character the author dazzles with a cacophony of words...."

The Bible, Old Testament: "A restless and tumultuous saga of a huge family... Bigger than *Roots*... Adventures in The Red Sea... The passions of Ruth... Jezebel and lust rekindled in middle age... the toll of the wilderness and the cry of Isaiah... the clash of men at arms in a struggle to win a homeland and a Father...."

The Bible, New Testament: "Not since the legendary *Studs Lonigan* has a book so captured the turmoil and struggle of a young blue collar worker.

SUPPORT YOUR LOCAL GRIFFIN

The griffin is an exotic creature composed of one-half lion, one-half eagle. Because of these mixed media, ornithologists are in disagreement about the griffin.

You will not, for example, find the griffin listed in *The Sibley Guide to Birds*. This is a pure piece of arrogance on the part of the National Audubon Society... but then, the society does not recognize the pterodactyl, either.

I am getting a little sick of people running around ignoring the griffin. And the pterodactyl. And, even, the unicorn. I am tired as all-get-out of people who go around hollering about bears (oh, pah, bears), and rhinos they have tamed (oh, tish, rhinoceros), and platinum blondes (oh, yawn). When someone tells me that he keeps sharks in his hot tub I am bored. I detest this continuing sophism that would convince us that the mamba is in every way superior to the common hoop snake. Fah. Give me a sensible, well-ordered hoop snake any time.

The whole sorry problem is caused by this century's craze for science. People think that everything must be explained. They want every creature catalogued, embalmed in museums, put on display... and named Alfred. People believe that if science cannot show them a griffin, then griffins do not exist.

Well, smarties, you are now in trouble. One of my best friends is a griffin. He lives in my chimney and his name is Hector. Hector is a magic griffin. He can shrink himself to about the size of a doughnut, and he can puff himself up to around the girth of your average rocket ship.

When he is doughnut-sized he looks a lot like my pet cat. When he is rocketing, the whole town nigh gets blown away in the wind from his wings. This, as anyone around here can tell you, usually happens in winter.

Hector will be exactly 2600 years old next Tuesday. I am giving him a party. The guests will be a couple of hoop snakes named Gloria and Lester, plus a unicorn named Uzz, and three pterodactyls named Prester John, Caligula, and Sam.

For his birthday Hector is getting an evil charm purchased (after a lot of mayhem) from an obscure tribe in Australia. Hector needs that charm because he is just too good-natured. In 2600 years, and with all the opportunity in the world, Hector has eaten no more than 400 to 500 politicians. It is scarcely enough. He knows it. He knows that I know it. It is the only dark secret in his life that will make him blush.

At first he tried to alibi. He claimed that the average politician has such bad taste... but, of course, that is no excuse. Anyone who lives for 2600 years cannot think it can be done without a certain amount of suffering.

There are advantages to associating with a griffin. For one thing, you never have chimney fires. Every time Hector fluffs up his feathers, and gives his tail a twitch, stuff tumbles out of that chimney faster than banalities at a Sunday School picnic.

In addition, griffins are interesting company. Having lived so long, Hector, even with his flaws, can tell you that a Republican tastes the same as a Commissar, and a Democrat greatly resembles a six-week's dead camel.

I think we should all quit thinking about bears, and begin thinking about griffins. To push this idea, I am proclaiming the week before election as National Griffin Week. Support your local griffin, friends. It may be out last chance.

ISRAEL AND ERNEST

The room was cold and the first wind of autumn rattled the window and there was death in that wind which was beautiful and also very sad. Shake, shake, went a hand, and then it went rattle, rattle. I moaned and a voice moaned back.

"Depart Israel," I said. "It is three o'clock in the morning and the truth of that is dark and severe, although, of course, it is also beautiful and very sad."

"Up!" Israel hollered.

"… when the sun rises. For now it is three o'clock in the morning."

"Moan," he said. (For those who do not know him, Israel is the ghost whose job it is to haunt my house. He haunts my house beautifully and very truly and well. He is wonderfully good at the haunting and we have been through much together).

"That did it," he said. "That did it, that did-dit."

"Did what, hombre?"

He slapped me awake. "You have to quit reading Hemingway before going to sleep," he explained. "And," he added thoughtfully, "you got to get rid of the damndog."

"Oooof," I added. "At three o'clock in the morning?" I yawned. Then a flicker of white drifted across the room. It was luminescent. It panted as it drifted.

"Arrrr..." I screamed, "a Ghost."

"Where?" Israel yelped and made a dive to get under the bed. Israel is scared silly of ghosts.

"There," I shrieked and pointed. The flicker of white slathered and simpered. It drooled and wagged its invisible tail. It seemed to bounce on its hind legs even if it did not have any. Then the flicker of white nuzzled closer and I began to sneeze.

"Oi," Israel moaned. "They fool me too, and there are tons of them. You have failed me once too often, kid. I'm moving."

"Don't leave me," I whimpered. "What is it?"

"Dog shed," he said. "The dog you so proudly brought home is shedding. Explain yourself."

"A long story."

"I have until dawn."

"A friend downtown...." I began.

"Search for the woman," he interrupted.

"All right," I said. "I met a lady friend downtown. She told me that I was a crude man who owned cats and wrote nothing but cat stories. She said I was sarcastic about dogs."

"Is she pretty?"

"They all are," I sobbed. "Even the ones who are dog lovers. Or maybe them, especially."

"You fool," Israel laughed. "You blighted idiot. This is too much." He rolled around on the floor whooping and laughing. "Jerk," he giggled. "So to impress a lady you bought a dog and a bunch of Hemingway novels...."

"Nothing in the books say a word about shed," I protested. "They are brave and true books and they say nothing about shed."

"I've changed my mind," Israel told me. "I'm not leaving. I'm staying around to see you handle this mess."

"I'll handle it all right. Yes sir. No-doubt-about-it."
But, I knew I was in trouble. "I'll learn about dogs and
write dog stories and all my readers will know that I am
fair and just and not simply a friend of cats."

"Two questions," Israel said. "First, what does a
Hemingway dog look like?"

"Lean and ranging and intelligent and serious and
brave."

"Second question. And you brought home a
Samoyed?"

"Yes."

"You see the difference?"

"That's three questions," I protested. "But, yes, I
see the difference. At least I see it now."

"Go back to sleep," Israel told me. "Tomorrow I'll
teach you to roll over and fetch... and how to use a
vacuum."

THE TIME THAT
TIME FORGOT

...Ah, love, let us be true
To one another! for the world, which seems
To lie before us like a land of dreams,
So various, so beautiful, so new,
Hath really neither joy, nor love, nor light,
Nor certitude, nor peace, nor help for pain;
And we are here as on a darkling plain
Swept with confused alarms of struggle and strife
Where ignorant armies clash by night.

from *Dover Beach* by Matthew Arnold

I

Through a random cast of ancient humors, or the almighty hand of God; or perhaps only the whim of indifferent Nature, some souls are given to wander widely while the cautious stay at home. We walk the nights, look down unending roads, and the universe stands before us cold as a harsh thought; though speckled with the stares of stars.

Thus it was in our youth when we went to war, and so it remained in this year of 1879 when we three, Charles Hare, Ephriam Miller, and I, Jonathan Light, arrived in these wet mountains of southeast America. Wanderers three, we proceeded in the name of Science, although by our natures we would, science or no, come exploring.

Rumors about time a-shifting, and ghosts, and power rose from these hills and stretched as far away as comfortable Baltimore from which we departed with mixed emotions. The greatest war in history is still vile memory. Baltimore abounds with former Confederate officers seeking new professions. Congress has failed America. It manufactures frenzies, although most of our people wish only reconciliation.

No doubt it was war that originally caused rumors about this land. Some fleeing Yankee or Reb stumbled into these valleys, and stumbled away, shrieking.

When we departed Baltimore our interest was ethnology. It is a young science, much praised these days in press, but cursed from pulpit. Our subject: a people living in these remote mountains where time seems skewed and wondrous. In 1879 there exists unexplained movement in skies and forest. The movement is always seen through mist, and whether it be animal or machine we did not at first know. There also exists a civilization that, for all intents, still lives in the 14th or 15th century. And, among the natives of this land are ancients who have power. We now know that the power is fabulous.

Rumors about shifting time, and ghosts, caught the attention of Charles Hare, our captain who is wealthy and could finance this trip. Charles is usually modest enough and, during the war, brave enough. He has a gentleman's persuasion about ethnology, and an English-y face not a little like his horse. His hair is brown and mane-like, his hands nearly as blunt as hooves. When he sits his horse one thinks of fox hunts and aristocracy.

Ephriam Miller, on the other hand, is near opposite. A down-easter of lower persuasions, in his native Maine he is known as a drinker and a brawler. He is also a ship maker and sailor who lives on the bare edge of respectability. During the war he was a Bosun. He is built like a massive barrel, but the girth is muscle and not fat. He is a man too cheery for the grim coast of Maine because he laughs with joy as he fights. He stands for drinks when he wins. No one has ever seen him lose.

And I, Jonathan Light, am quiet, bookish, and a recorder of this adventure. Before the war I worked for newspapers and perhaps read too many adventure tales by gentlemanly Englishmen. While I make no great noise about it, and sometimes regret the truth; fact is that I am too large for a man of books, too strong. A circus once tried to hire me as a giant. A man of my size does not need to say "no" more than once. Unlike our friend Ephriam, I no longer enjoy battle because I've killed too many. I sometimes enjoy laughing.

These valleys are not easily found. When we arrived in Asheville and completed our outfit with stores of flour and salt and tobacco, local people denied knowledge of this place. They thought us northern intruders, or, as likely, did not wish to think of what lies in these mountains and valleys. Asheville presents a closed and aristocratic society, self-anointed. In Asheville time proceeds, clock-like, day after tranquil day. It is always respectable. It does not wind around or turn upon itself.

We departed Asheville in late April, three men, five horses and a mule. We carried .44 Colt revolvers and the new 45-70 rifles with a wealth of cartridges.

Now it is early August. One horse lies dead. The mule walks overloaded. The animals put a strain on our situation. We buy hay and a little corn at an occasional hill farm, but mostly depend on forage. Thus, the animals are not thrifty. Ephriam and I could do without them; but about horses, Charles is adamant.

Trails are few and we descend or ascend carefully. Our remaining horses snort and hesitate when entering a trail. They show the good sense of large animals in dangerous territory. And, although we are experienced adventurers we also hesitate before this immensity of forest. Streams run from every hill, crystalline and noisy. Ancient mountains rise mist-clad, round-shouldered, and worn by an eternity of weather.

The horse was stricken in the midst of storm. We
had seen the sites of other strikes, but took them for
the results of lightning; because, in this wet land lightning walks the hills on forked legs. Lightning here is
common as mist, and mist is common as air. Only
during afternoons of full sun does the mist withdraw.

There is no arguing with these storms. Thunder
rolls across mountaintops, booms through valleys, and
rain sheets before wind no less than in a storm at sea.
We huddle in waterproofs and beneath canvas if in
the field. Otherwise, we seek shelter in a cave where
we have established camp.

It was at the camp the horse died. It stood
hobbled with the others. The animals grazed until
the arrival of storm, then moved toward each other
as thunder crashed like cannon, and rain turned their
hides bright.

The doomed mare stood in the center of the little
herd. Suddenly, surprised, she fell as silently as night
wings. The other horses screamed, edged aside,
moved through mist like slow specters. The mare lay
with smoke rising from a furious wound. Even with
wind, ozone tainted the blowing mist. The carcass
lay still. No burns appeared on the other beasts.
Worse, no thunder followed. This stroke of light, or
lightning, walked in silence.

"Thunderation," Ephriam said. Then he said,
"Damn." Then he said, "Goddamn." He stood beside us in the mouth of the cave. Behind him the
cave stretched far back in darkness. Ephriam stood
in the cave's entry like a man framed in a shadow box.
"Chums, it's against nature. Where? What? Smell
the stink."

Charles stepped into the storm. "Unfortunate
beast. Poor animal." He walked through driving rain

to the horse, knelt, and touched the searing wound. He drew back his hand and blew on burned fingers. Then he rocked back on his heels heedless of rain and became a detached observer. His scientific interests are wide. While all three of us have inflicted hot wounds during the war, none of us, and doubtless no one else, had ever seen this kind of wound. It ran through the beast like a scorching razor.

The carcass was not halved. Rather, the strike hit directly from above. It struck between neck and shoulder, so that the head twisted awkwardly away. Bone gleamed hot and flesh cooked. Stench rose and rain pounded. We three stood beside the animal and fought justifiable fear.

"Think carefully. What did you see?" Charles, who is sometimes fastidious, sometimes finicky, wrinkled his nose at the smell of burned hair and bone.

"When lightning strikes," Ephriam mused, "there is always sound. There's a crack or a thump. There's always thunder. I didn't see nothin'. The important part is I didn't hear nothin'."

"We have witnessed hot damage elsewhere," I said. A week after departing Asheville we began seeing broken trees and broken rock holding the imprint of fire.

"Make complete notes," Charles told me. "Be assiduous."

My notes partially read: 'Light flashing like a bolt from Jehovah or Zeus. Bones sliced shear. Flesh instantly cooked.'

When the rain stopped we towed the carcass fifteen rods from camp. The horses wanted no dealings with the dead mare. They shied, but Charles is completely attuned to horses. Our tow left the dead mare near an animal trail. Scavengers would take care of the carcass.

These hills roll endless and rise to heights between five and six thousand feet. When standing on a high ridge one looks west and sees tops of mountains stretch to the horizon. There is history here, one worth knowing if we are to survive.

Forty-two years ago in the presidency of Andrew Jackson, peoples of this region, Cherokee and Creek and Catawba, were removed to the western territories. The removal was not gentle. Many died. Some escaped to these hills. They mixed with people already here, an odd mixture.

The resident people live in ancient ways. The refugees who fled Jackson's soldiers were accustomed to more modern ways. Before removal many Cherokee were wealthy. They owned businesses, farms, and slaves. They had a written language and a newspaper. Even though highly civilized, they still knew how to survive in these hills.

They survived because no army on earth is large enough or skilled enough to find someone hiding among these endless mountains. The very eye of God would become befuddled among these mists and valleys, among these smokes and rushing streams. And, there are spirits.

No ethnologist worth his salt would deny the presence of ghosts. For, although one may not believe in ghosts, one must accept that others do. Thus we walk in a fantastic land where the people we study have a great mythology. It is a mythology of ghosts and spirits and witches.

And, one must admit, although a few men may not believe in ghosts, it does not mean those men are not haunted. Each of our party carries memories of war. The dead and dying drift through our dreams; of which, perhaps, more later.

On the day when the horse died, and before disposing of the carcass, we returned to the cave as the storm slackened. August heat returned and the forest steamed. Giant trees formed a canopy holding heat to the ground.

"Reduce our knowledge to elements." Charles stripped wet clothing. He knelt quite naked as he searched his pack for dry gear. Charles appears gawkish without clothes. His upper body weighs heavy, his lower body light; like a workhorse on legs of a racehorse. To me, Charles said, "Make a written note." He did not say a record would be wanted by others if none of us survive.

My notes further read:
The Land
Wet with eternal mist
Movement in the sky but only in the mist
Movement on the landscape but only in the mist
Electrical storms of frequency and strength
Dense forest
Much game
Destructive strikes of light
The People
Reclusive
Matrilineal
Hostile. Doubtless warlike.
Primitive, but with occasional modern weapons acquired in aftermath of The War of the Rebellion.

. . . . . .

"Ain't likely the natives throw lightning bolts." Ephriam does not enjoy mysteries. "Seems like what happened ties to storm."

"Examine all possibilities," Charles told him. "It may tie to mist. It may tie to neither."

"As I understand it, " I suggested, "our first problem asks if these strikes are random, or planned. If planned, we face an unknown and dangerous opponent."

"Random, surely," Charles said. "Planning supposes a controlling presence. In which case, we would already be lost."

"Because," Ephriam growled, "folks in these parts are somewhat direct." His barrel-like figure seemed vague in the dim cave. His blue eyes shifted as he looked beyond the cave into the mist. Even at rest, and in an easily defended spot, Ephriam searched the forest for enemies. "Fair question. What do they think of you?" he asked me. "With them it sets up as either worship or kill."

When we first encountered the native people they fled before me. Men of my generation rarely stand six feet tall, and certainly not seven-six. Men of my generation may weigh, bone and muscle, fourteen stone but not twenty. The native people stand small beside Ephriam, are dwarfed beside me. They fled believing I am a monster or a creature of mythology.

One who did not run was a young woman. Early in June we paused, thinking ourselves unobserved, at the foot of a trail which ended at a confluence of two streams. The young woman attended a fish trap. She removed a catch of trout.

She dressed, as do all the ancient people, male and female, in deerskin apron with single strap across naked breast; the apron with numbers of carefully sewn pockets. People here carry their livings with them; flint, tobacco, pipes, knives and other small tools. In winter they cloak with furs.

"Beautiful sight," Charles breathed. "Nature's fair child."

"Beautiful fish," Ephriam muttered. "I'm wearied of venison. You reckon she'd trade? "

I wondered what crossed her mind as she turned and saw three strangers sitting massive horses. We must indeed have looked like creatures of myth. Charles is of average height, but larger than the native men. Ephriam has the girth of a sound tree, and I, a giant astride a giant horse. We expected her to fade quickly into forest as had others before her.

Instead, she stood quietly and watched with the calmness of power; the calm of a woman who knew she could harm if she wished, and could not be harmed. From the forest came the crashing of a heavy body, the snort of a bear. Mist blew across the streams. Damp warmth radiated from the forest.

"We witness courage," Charles said in a low voice. "Either hers or ours. We must speak to her."

Fragments of the English language survive. A primitive sign language exists. Before our departure from Baltimore we learned somewhat of Cherokee. Given time and patience we could communicate. I give the sum of our conversation, since phrase by phrase would be tedious.

"Why are you here? I don't want you." Her voice sounded low and no more friendly than her words. Her face was not as round as tribes of the far west. Her face seemed nearly European, brown eyes, tan skin, a face that would be lovely should she smile. I judged her as being in her middle 20s.

"We come in the name of science." Charles spoke softly.

"I do not know that word. It is not necessary. Your science is no good."

"There is much lightning here."

"It is the robe of Thunder."

In the forest the crashing of the bear told that it circled us. Bears have curiosity. They will follow a man for great distance, not stalking, just watching.

They walk silent when they wish, but this one did not wish, and it sounded huge.

"I want to know Thunder," Charles said. "Does one praise Thunder?" One learns of a people by learning of their Gods.

She looked at Charles as if she feared him hopelessly stupid. "You praise Thunder. You dance. Thunder laughs."

We would later understand that the natives teach by asserting the ludicrous. If, for example, a youngster does a foolish thing, he will be praised for doing well. The culture teaches with kindness, but with no small touch of sarcasm.

"Then Thunder is an enemy?"

"No."

"A friend?"

"No."

"What?"

"Thunder is."

We would also later understand that the natives accept existence of natural things without judging. To them a stream without trout pools is not worse than a stream with many pools. One is a stream with pools, one without, neither better or worse. Thus, Thunder is.

Charles looked to the skyline where round-shouldered mountains stood with tops covered by mist. Far off, in the mist, movement flashed in positive streaks of silver and orange. Orange bloomed like explosions, but there was no sound. Mist muffled sounds of forest and stream. Rapid and desperate movement came and went through the forest, as if killing forces confronted each other.

We all have memories of war. Memories of charges, battle flags flying and the screams of maddened or dying men, and dying horses. Perhaps our memories peopled the mist and the forest with sound-less battle.

Charles pointed upward but remained silent. The young woman stood content with her own thoughts. Soon she would decide we were no longer interest-ing. These people are direct. She would simply walk away.

"War?" Charles asked.

"You go away," she said. "Carry off all that you brought." She turned to leave.

"Let her go," I told Charles. "She'll say no more. Not at present."

......

In the days and weeks that followed, as June folded into July, and then to August, we feared we would become complacent with forms and colors that moved through mist. Patterns developed. On days when mist was cut by storm, and when rain fell with violence, colors on mountain tops flared high. Because of mist, red explosions appeared as orange smears, and flashes of blue light turned silver. Sometimes ozone drifted through the rain. We would later discover a wrecked tree, seared and smoking.

On noons when mist retreated before August sun, movement in the forest fragmented. We could see figures of men ghosting from tree to tree and some-times meeting. The figures were nebulous. No one could actually say he saw battles, but could not say he saw anything else.

We often went to the confluence of streams hop-ing for the return of the young woman. Instead, our adventure took a different shape. Natives concluded that while we might be demons we were not presently dangerous. We were approached by delegates of two separate camps.

The first was a warrior who appeared out of mist. He moved easily and without fear. He wore gray pants of a kind that I had seen on many a dead Confederate, and linen shirt, worn but serviceable. He carried a cap-and-ball rifle, and a steel knife. This warrior had a broad Indian forehead combined with negroid features. His skin was chocolate colored, his hair kinky, a statement of other important history.

In the American south, from the first visits of negroid and caucasoid peoples, there has been much interchange with the native population. The ethnologist who hopes to find an unmixed culture is overly optimistic. However, because of the ancient peoples there was some reason for optimism. This warrior, though, was modern.

He was clearly an experienced man. His rifle was shouldered muzzle down. His moccasins were worn without being worn through, which showed that he knew how to move with admirable economy. Moccasins would not have lasted our party for a week. His rifle is now out-moded, but muzzleloaders were serviceable during the War of the Rebellion. Doubtless, like us, he had fought. He stood nearly as tall as Ephriam and he moved with the light steps of a man who can walk soundless through dry leaves. Such woodsmen drift like spirits through the forest.

"No need to fear," he said most pleasantly. "I'm not the Fool Killer." His English was as good as ours, but slightly nasal. It held hints of cultivated speech, the soft and often dangerous sort one finds in Norfolk. He approached three well-armed men. He actually reassured three experienced men. His confidence set us aback.

"No fools here," Charles said easily.

"The mule ain't too bright... but got a trick or

two in his withers." Ephriam moved two steps away from Charles. If a fight was to happen it would be stupid to remain clustered.

"Next time you get to town," the warrior told Ephriam, "shop around and buy a sense of humor." He grinned openly. "You gents are serious beyond moderate." He searched the forest behind us. "On t'other hand, you've got a right. You have stepped into a hell of a fix."

"Charles Hare," Charles said, introducing himself. Then he introduced Ephriam. I introduced myself.

"Bester," the warrior said. "Albert Bester." He gave his white name. No Indian would give his real name to strangers. We were forced to wonder if Bester actually was Indian, or only had the blood. Lots of Cherokee and Catawba had abandoned Indian ways for white civilization. And, where had he acquired hints of cultivation?

"... a helluva fix," Ephriam asked. "Which one? It looks like we got enough to fill a main'sl."

"Why are you here? I'm not just curious. Your answer is important." Bester stood casually but not at rest. He rested his rifle, but did not lean on it.

Charles explained and Bester at first seemed amused. Then a sense of unease entered the situation.

"If only you were hunting gold, or trapping fur, or stealin' children, I'd know what to tell you." Bester mused. "The people in these parts have handled such matters for nigh on three centuries." He actually seemed puzzled. "Don't you have enough trouble with your own world?"

We figured then that Bester was Indian, or at least mostly. The spirit of science is alien to Indian vision. Tools, yes. Inventions, yes. But systematic inquiry toward a nebulous or unknown end, no. One cannot understand the notion of *is* and inquire about *maybe*.

"We do have enough trouble," Charles admitted. "If we look at someone else's world we may find ways of fixing our own." His simple explanation didn't cover all the facts, but covered enough.

Bester smiled in the quiet and cultivated manner of the best southern society: here he was, Indian, negro, a rough and tumble woodsman; and yet when he wanted he could put on the ways of the white aristocrat. Quite an actor. "Tell of your success."

"We're eating well," Ephriam said, "and wearing out our boots."

"We early on understood that we would have to establish camp and wait for people to come to us." Charles watched the forest where movement had ceased with the appearance of Bester. "If we enter villages without invitation we would be seen as intruders."

"Odd thing to hear from a Yankee," Bester said quietly. There was cloaked anger in his voice. "Nobody invited Grant and Sherman."

"We explore on foot," Charles explained. "One man always stays in camp to attend the animals."

"Because," Ephriam muttered, "horses have a way of wanderin'."

"They have a way of getting stolen," Bester said. "Renegades take them. Say what you mean."

"The funny thing is..." Ephriam told him, "... I like you. You've already jumped my hide twice, and damn if I still don't like you."

"You made a good scheme," Bester told Charles. "Had you entered a village you would have been treated well, then killed on return to camp." Bester looked toward the forest. "Three forces exist here, and all three can handle you."

Bester explained that a village of Cherokee, adequately armed, held territory a few miles to the southwest. Native people, the people from whom the Cherokee had risen, held territories scattered through the mountains. Although a certain amount of tribal interchange was possible, the groups pretty much went their own ways and ignored each other.

A third force came from medicine known only to a few of the original natives, the ancient people. Such people used power rarely. "But," Bester explained, "they can bend nature to their purpose. Their own people revere and fear them, my people mostly fear them, and you would do well to be mortally afraid. Nature guards them."

I thought of the young woman we had met back in June. I thought of the crashing of the bear in the forest. A huge bear.

"And the strikes of light and fire? Are those a manifest of nature? We've already lost one horse."

"They come from the west," Bester told Charles, "and people don't go there. However, it's what I want to chew over with you."

According to Bester the strikes of fire began during the war, but never amounted to much. In these endless hills war otherwise made little impression. Life walked day by day and night by night, the unending circle of time the Indian knows. Skirmishes between small groups occasionally ended in the death of a warrior, or the kidnapping of a child. For the most part seasons rolled. Corn crops and tobacco and pumpkins grew and were harvested. Rumors of war penetrated the hills and some men walked off in the direction of battle, to return with stories of exploits that might or might not be true. And, of course, a good many did not return.

"We see dead men moving through the forest,"

Bester said. "Lots more lately. Strikes of fire increase. You might say things are no longer casual."

"We see them also."

"Most likely, you see spirits," Bester said. "Spirits fill this land. People live beside spirits and don't much care, because spirits only live on the edge of the world. The ghosts are a different matter." Bester tapped his rifle butt against the ground. He now seemed a little dangerous, and very sad. "A ghost is the shape of someone who made bad mistakes. Folks here live in established ways. We fear mistakes."

"Spirits on the edge of this world? Are they part of tales we hear about time? Are spirits from another time?" Charles tried to sound casual, but it was a failure. His excitement at getting new information got the best of him.

"What is your experience?" Bester asked. "Something has misfired. Something is cockeyed. What's the date?"

"August 14th, 1879," I replied. When one keeps a record, one always knows the date.

"It probably is August," Bester said, "because it smells like August. But what is this?" He fished in a pocket and pulled out a small piece of material. It was flat and hardened like fired clay, but without the graininess of clay. "Came from the sky," Bester said. "Plunked into a stream. Rattled people."

The fragment showed cracks and a burn. It measured no more than two inches square, and affixed to it was a very small, colored cylinder with soldered wire.

"A raven or a jay had to have dropped it, but what in blazes is it?"

"Came from the sky?"

"I know what you're thinking," Bester told Charles, "because I already thought my way down that trail. But only birds fly. It's either a bird or a sky god."

"Fire on the mountaintops," Charles said. "Always to the west?"

"Up until now."

"And what comes from the east?" Charles looked toward the east. "I ask, because if we look west, it pays to know what's at our backs." He let the business of sky gods pass. Time enough to inquire about superstitions later.

Toward the east the sun had cleared the mountaintops an hour after first light. Mist rolled into valleys and hollows. In two more hours sun would begin to drive the mist upward. The forest would lose some of its green glitter as mist dried from leaves and needles.

"Ghosts and Yankees," Bester said. "Dead Confederates. Ghosts come from the east. They also drift this way from Georgia."

"Have there always been ghosts?"

"Here and there," Bester said. "Lots more of them lately. They hover around men like you. And men like me." Bester turned the broken fragment over and over in his hand. The colored cylinder, orange and blue, contrasted with his dark skin. "Men like you won't believe this next, and I could give damn less, but tell you anyhow."

He told of buffalo ghosting along trails, although forest buffalo disappeared from these parts two hundred years ago. He told of Spanish adventurers in search of gold, and, although gold has been found in these hills the native people never valued it. He told of murder, rape, retaliation; told of the ghosts of history. "Sometimes," he concluded, "it's like three hundred years never passed."

"It's always been this way?"

"Only a little... lots more of late. Spanish came into these parts in the 16th century. Sometimes they're

still here. It's like nothing is ever lost, which is un-
natural." Bester looked eastward, shrugged, and pre-
sented us with an explanation. His notion seemed
simple enough, but none of us had thought of such a
thing. Bester claimed that in normal history — as
opposed to what was going on — every time you gain
something, you lose something. Sometimes you lose
something good.

"You have new Springfields," he said about our
rifles. "You can extract and load in two seconds. I
can load in ten seconds. You gain time, but you lose
dexterity." He looked toward our horses; two roans,
two blacks, one with a white star. "Around here people
picked up mobility when they got horses. Some folks
can't live without. Other people understood that they
lost freedom if they adopted horses... which is why
plenty people don't have 'em."

He was correct, of course. Horses take too much
time and care.

"Which means," said Bester, "that I'm quicker than
you, and freer than you; and I live without horse dung
and horse flies. You, on the other hand, can travel
further and load faster."

"I understand," Charles said, and he did. It was
not a novel idea, only sensible. "What we have is
handy in war and adventure, but limits us in everyday
life. Gain and loss."

Bester looked at the fragment of unknown material which looked foreign in his hand. He looked west.
"There are some gains a man don't need. Something
showed up during the war. I want it defeated. We
can handle Spanish, be they ghosts or real, but fire
on the hills and strikes in the forest...." He looked at
Charles as if wondering whether we were good
enough. "Somebody has to plug a leak in history. I'll
venture it, but could use some extra rifles."

We all looked west. One rifle, or four, seemed feeble if what we saw was what it seemed.

"Keep explaining," Ephriam told Bester. "Them explosions is matter for comment."

"If they are explosions we'll know in time to turn back. I don't fret the explosions. What I fret is whether you gents are causing the leak." Bester laid a hand on Ephriam's shoulder, like friend to friend. "You haven't been here. All you know is you've lost a horse. I've been here, and the price of this lantern show has already gone from a plug-nickel to six-bits."

"And you'll solve it with rifles?" Charles was intrigued. Our sense of adventure had brought us to this place, and so far there had been no adventure. I entertained doubts.

"For defense and for game," Bester said. "If history is skewed we scout and find the cause. If we can't cure it we come back."

"Or not." Ephriam looked wary, like a boat thrown ashore, and wondering what was to become of itself.

Charles looked at me, at Ephriam. "We're having little luck here."

"We got an extra horse," Ephriam admitted.

"Bring the horses, but be prepared to trade or lose them. Or trade them now," Bester told Charles. "Shank's mare before this finishes.

"Why?"

"This is mountain country and not a field of battle." He pointed to the depths of the surrounding forest. "From lookin' at your plunder, I expect you gents were damned fine soldiers, but stealth is wanted. It's different territory."

"I'm a sailor," Ephriam told him, and for the first time, in a long time, looked at ease. "Don't lump me with these cannoneers."

"We'll be ready in two days," Charles said. "Rendezvous day after tomorrow."

......

Our second visitor stepped from the forest so quietly we did not know she was there. A horse whin-
nied. Stomped. Then stilled. An old, old woman
moved toward us. She wore copper ornaments and a
cape of raven feathers. Her face, though heavily
wrinkled, showed relationship to the young woman
we had met at the fish trap. I would have wagered
this was the grandmother. It was as if the young
woman had turned ancient. The grandmother, doubtless.

She carried a polished and ornamented stick, possibly for use as a cane. Possibly ceremonial. Possibly
both.

We extended full respect. This woman lived in
ways made possible through the seclusion of these
hills. Either that, or time truly was bent. From her
world the Cherokee, far, far back in time, had derived.
She was not Cherokee, but the mother of the Cherokee; an important fact. These Indians trace family
relationships from the mother. A few of the women
are reputed to have great power. This woman could
live in ancient ways because she was so strong she
needed no gun, no steel knife, no missionaries.

"You walk west," she said. "What do you know?
You better know a lot."

I could nearly feel Charles' thrill. Here was a person who we had traveled far to see. This woman could
tell every custom, every tale, of the world of the 16th
century. This woman's world differed in no large respect from the world when Hernado DeSoto landed
in 1539.

"I know a little bit," Charles said. "You know

more."

If an experienced man looked at our horses and outfit with disdain, we would be alarmed. Bester, though, had thought well enough of them. This woman looked at our camp and was displeased. "Bester is plenty smart. You do what Bester says."

When he left, Bester had disappeared to the south. This old woman came from the north. It was unlikely they had met. Her opinion of our camp caused me to worry.

Our rifles were stacked. She looked at them. "You don't want better guns. You want no guns." She looked west. "Plenty guns there." From the forest came a loud snort. A bear. A big bear.

"Thunder lives there. Thunder can take care of himself. Don't go troubling Thunder."

Charles looked at me, and the look meant — *don't* miss a word. Document everything.

"War lives there," the woman said. "He moves this way. You stop him." Her wrinkled face remained tranquil, but her eyes belied the face. They were afire with anger. "War has plenty medicine," she told us. "I have plenty medicine. I send medicine with Bester. You do what Bester says." She walked back into the forest.

Charles stood irresolute. He wanted to follow her, and knew he should not.

"What did she mean?" Ephriam asked. "No guns. What in raging hell did she mean?"

"We now have strong evidence that time is skewed. Surely, that woman cannot be of the 19th century." Charles looked west. "Better guns? No guns? If time is misfiring, do we see the future in the west? He shook his head, as if to relieve himself of crazy thoughts. "Impossible. Impossible. In that direction madness lies."

"No guns at all," Ephriam insisted. "What in the name of all that is wonderful did she mean, 'no guns'."

"If necessary I will fight to defend us," I said, "and I expect I'll fight to defend her; but by all gods great and small do not expect me to initiate an attack."

I could see by their manners that my comrades agreed. In an ugly past, Charles and I stood side by side watching men fall before our cannon. At long range we loaded shot, and as range closed we loaded canister. When we ran out of canister we loaded broken glass, rocks, and horseshoe nails. Our field piece was like a giant scattergun.

When overrun we met bayonets with clubs and knives. Ephriam, although he does not discuss it, had waded through scuppers running with blood, had seen blood splash so high that it discolored sails.

"The man is a Reb and dangerous," Ephriam said about Bester.

"And I'm a Northern and dangerous," I told him.

II

That night after the old woman left was a night of dreams. Charles took the first watch, I the second, and Ephriam the chill hours of night to dawning. The forest seemed alive with movement, and our fire at the mouth of the cave drew cold air from within. Chill circled our backs.

When I settled in the dreams began. I once more saw men run through smoke from our guns, saw the twist and fall of bodies, heard Rebel yells sharp as the call of eagles. I relived my own most horrible event of the war.

It happened on a wet day in mud. Rain had stopped. Sun glared hot as a forge, and muggy heat pressed white smoke from black powder to the ground. Smoke clung to earth like thickest fog. Rebel yells sounded an attack, and our supporting riflemen fired into the smoke as we loaded canister. Out there in the smoke men died by hundreds and we were glad. We saw little. Mostly, we only heard them dying. What we saw was smoke, and mud as liquid as a hog pen.

Tongues of flame leapt from our guns, and we had occasional glimpses of falling men, like spirits in sweltering mist. Mud threatened to silence our cannon, foul the fuse, and our cannon kept trying to bury itself on recoil. Mud sucked at the gun as I lifted it. Only my great strength kept it free and pointed.

Further down the line came the sound of a breakthrough and Rebel cheering. Then, through smoke, we heard the panting of attacking men. They were not yelling now, but sloughing through mud with bayonet and sword and pistol. They pressed forward in the face of canister, and canister swept holes in their gray and tattered line. One by one our guns stopped firing, felled either by mud or Confederates.

Then the Rebs were on us. An artillerist's hell. Charles stood with pistol and sword, and I emptied my rifle. A man jerked and fell, his face twisting in astonishment. There was no time to reload. I used the rifle as a club.

A boy, hardly more than a child, appeared out of smoke. He was small, tow-headed, with brown and excited eyes. He wore a red rag at his throat, a lucky piece probably torn from a scarf made by his mother. In his right hand he carried a cavalry saber. His left hand spurted blood; fingers gone. The boy was not yet aware that he was wounded. He stumbled from the smoke, stopped amazed when he saw me, and for a moment, hesitated. In the dread heat of battle I must have looked like a giant risen out of smoke and ancient tales. He was entitled to run. He was fourteen, at most. He was too brave.

I struck with the rifle butt, slamming it sideways against his left arm. He spun, nearly dropped the saber, nearly fell from the blow. He staggered, looked at his left hand, and looked at me in disbelief. He believed it was I who had wounded him. The wound pumped blood that spattered and mixed in mud. He was already as good as dead but seemed not to know it.

He staggered forward with saber pointed, a dead boy trying to kill a still living man. With the butt of the rifle I broke his skull and saved him having to watch his life flow away into mud.

A boy. Fourteen, at best. A boy no doubt dead because of cheap romance. He had imagined he would excel in war. He had imagined himself a victor. A boy, and not a very big one. Nothing to be done about it then. Nothing to be done about it later. Men running through smoke, ghosting through smoke. It was war; and may Abe Lincoln and Jeff Davis, and all abolitionists and slavers, and all cotton men and industrialists, roast in everlasting hell.

When I awoke, jerked out of dreams by terror and no small guilt, the sun had not yet walked the top of the eastern mountains. My head hurt. I watched my companions. Subdued. No one talked about dreams.

I almost trust Charles, almost. His judgement was sound during battle, and surely it was sound on this occasion. Ephriam almost trusted Charles. Neither of us trusted Bester.

Charles had allied with Bester, and Bester was a Reb. Perhaps Charles could forgive the war but I could not. Hard to tell about Ephriam... likely, with Ephriam, it was the same.

And, Bester, part Indian and part Afric, was not necessarily of a mood to cherish the company of Yankees. It would be hard for him to forgive the rapes and fires and total destruction of the war. Besides, Bester was an enigma. Why would a man of his race have done battle in behalf of the south?

It was with large suspicion, and larger misgiving that I spent the day helping to cache supplies in the fond hope they would not be stolen. We then loaded a bit of salt, sugar, and flour on the horses. We packed a few items for trade, steel knives and, more desirable, flat files to keep knives sharp. We struck south to the Cherokee village where we were first greeted in sullen silence. When the purpose of our visit became clear, the Indians professed friendliness which we knew was a lie.

We traded for Indian tobacco — strong as a drug and used as medicine — and for other medicines. We returned to camp knowing that each would carry only a knife, a rifle, a revolver, a blanket, Lucifer matches waterproofed with paraffin, coffee, a little tea; a pot or a skillet. Additional gear would be packed by mule, but we did not know how long we would own horses and mule.

"And so," Charles said at sundown, "we commit to chance, or God, or a Johnny Reb who may be saint or rascal."

"You can commit to him all you want," Ephriam told Charles. "Me, I'm still figgerin'."

"Rascal, no doubt," I said, "but no damned saint."

The fire before the mouth of the cave glowed with small but positive energy. From the western hills came the rumble of Thunder.

In the second night of dreams strange beasts appeared, winged and fanged and unlovely; beasts of the apocalypse. Hordes of people fled along trails. From the depths of forest came echoes and strange cries, the sound of weeping, wails of such high pitch one thought only of wounds.

Disembodied faces appeared, fleshy, smooth-shaven, speaking harsh language. Jowly faces with cruel eyes. Then the faces grew bodies and uniforms, generals and tyrants, epaulets and medals dangling; those symbols of ribbon and brass that power awards itself, symbols intended to persuade the foolish that there is merit in much that is damnable.

I awoke to the sound of a heavy body crashing in the forest. My first thought was of the horses, but knew that Ephriam would be alert and attending. The heavy sound seemed somehow comforting. I stirred coals and rebuilt the fire; venison, biscuit and coffee. Charles and Ephriam packed remaining gear for the long road. Not much said. We listened to occasional crashing in the forest and stared into mist.

"If we go to defeat war," I said, "then I'll play the game." I did not explain why I said it, and my comrades did not ask questions. "If this was just a pleasure jaunt I would not." They still did not ask.

Bester appeared from the forest as naturally as a stream runs. We heard no sound. The horses gave no alarm. He still carried the muzzleloader but was now dressed in deerskin. We, having no deerskin, had packed waterproofs. He looked over our gear even before greeting us. Bester was not a man given to wasting words.

"An old woman visited." His was not a question. He squatted before the fire, refused food, accepted coffee that was boiled and black. "Panther piss," he said with satisfaction, and by way of compliment.

He seemed less a creature of mist or history. These woodsmen are practical fellows, but their stealth often makes them seem insubstantial. "The old woman said what?"

"She sends strong medicine with you," Charles

told him. Charles searched the forest. "I don't understand medicine. Do you carry it, or is it with that bear?"

"If you saw it," Bester said, "it would likely look like a bear. I think you'll never see it."

"Medicine?"

"She commands nature," Bester told us, "and don't ask how because I don't know." On this day his voice did not sound like the white aristocracy of Virginia. His voice held the same quiet, but with little accent. He sounded like a man wise in his job, but also wise enough to use caution. I wondered how cautious he felt he had to be around us.

"She said don't take better guns, take no guns," Ephriam told him. "Do you know about that?"

"You'd be amazed how much I don't know. What that woman understands was lost by everybody else two hundred years ago. Hang onto your rifles."

We followed a west-running trail. In these parts the lumbermen have still not struck. Giant trees rose in protected hollows and along streams. The broad trail skirted the base of mountains. In these hills are trails, paths, and great trails. Important to know the difference.

A path is well worn, short, and leads somewhere; a confluence of streams, an Indian ballfield of rough and dangerous games, or ceremonial site. Trails are different. Some trails follow the paths of animals, then extend beyond those paths. Some trails are made, hacked out, walked over, brush pushed aside; easily overgrown if not used. The trail we followed was a great trail used for war or trading. We moved without stealth, following Bester's lead.

We felt that we moved through a timeless landscape. We stood guard through nights of owl-call and the ticking of death-watches; and whether those death-watch insects existed in the night, or only ticked in our memories, none could say. We trekked, camped, slept, woke, trekked. Twice we waited as Bester reconnoitered an Indian camp, and twice we skirted that camp. Indians scouted us from the forest, and we could not know if they were alive or spectral. Bester remained alert, as did we all. We were soldiers moving through strange terrain.

A week into the forest, and with Thunder booming in the west, the trail crested a small rise and descended into a shrouded valley. Nature, herself, seemed to change and grow dark. Orange smears of fire flashed in western hills.

Mist covered the trail. Ravens sat silent on low branches like black smudges on mist. The birds did not call, or chortle, or shriek.

"Soul catchers," Bester said about the ravens. "Spirits. You never get a squawk from them until some fool goes to glory."

Deer bounced across the trail and chipmunks clung to trees, watching. The chipmunks did not scold. A panther stood silent beside the trail. Our horses saw nothing, or at least did not respond. They passed the panther as if it were not there.

"Nary a snort," Ephriam said to Charles, and it sounded like a question.

"Because the beasts can't smell or see it," Charles said. "I can't smell it. I doubt my senses."

"Soul catchers?" Ephriam said to Bester. Ephriam did not sound scientific. He sounded like a sailor, and sailors are almost always superstitious.

"Hang tight to what soul you've got," Bester said. "Those birdies don't jest." To Charles, he said, "Spirits aren't our problem. Trouble lies t'other side of yon hill."

In the next valley a south-running stream crashed

overfilled and dangerous because of August storms. Water tore at banks. Water backed up, and young poplars stood in water. Trees bent before current. We would have to move north, or south, in order to find a place to ford.

As we waited on Bester's lead the horses made small snorts and caught the jitters. The mule flat-out brayed.

"Hunker down," Ephriam said as he headed for cover. We automatically put our horses on tether between us and the hillside. The horses tried to shy from the hill. The mule went wide-eyed. During the war, mules had a reputation for frenzy in combat. This mule lived up to it. It tried to shake its load.

"I'm puttin' trust in not much these days, but I trust horses." Ephriam took his rifle off half-cock as he knelt behind a massive oak.

"Raiders," Bester muttered toward the hill. "They want the horses and rifles. I reckon they've got more'n their share of surprise coming." He turned away from the hill and toward the stream. We heard his weapon cock.

While Bester covered our rear we faced the hillside. Blood churns hot and fast at such moments. It's hard to stand easy, but it pays nothing to court excitement. We heard the report of Bester's rifle at the same moment we heard a flat explosion, almost a pop.

Bester knelt and faced the stream. Ephriam continued to scan the hillside as, at the report, Charles and I turned to Bester. On the tree behind which Charles had knelt, a black rock hit, then fell harmless to the ground. There were lots of such rocks around, and in all sizes. They were smoothed by rolling in the streams.

From across the stream a small puff of smoke

showed where our assailant had been, for surely by now he had moved. I turned my rifle toward the stream.

"Find him," Ephriam said over his shoulder, "because you'll be looking at one dead Sadducee."

Charles reached down, feeling for the rock that hit the tree. He kept searching while watching the forest on the other side of the stream. His hand felt here, there, and found no rock. He turned back to the hill while we continued to face the stream.

"Already dead," Bester told Ephriam, "and he's been just that dead for at least three hundred years." Bester did not relax but he took his time reloading. "Keep a watch for anything ornery," he told us, "though likely all you'll see is smoke. We'll soon be watching a skirmish."

"You shot at what?" Charles did not lower his weapon. He kept it pointed across the creek.

"I saw movement that might have been alive," Bester said quietly, "A picket is a picket."

"Rocks," I said, "not shot?"

"Maybe from a wheel-lock." Bester sounded tired. "You can't hit damn-all with them, but you can load anything that fits in the barrel. And make that a massacre, not a skirmish." He looked to the hillside, then across the swollen stream. "If they were shooting rocks they were out of shot. Meantime, those raiders are among the living. They're after us, but they're about to catch a case of the dreadfuls. They'll scamper like hares."

I wish I could say that what followed was a mere tableau, the carefully constructed scene, and the short vision so popular in society these days. Instead, this became one more lick of fire from the Devil's furnace.

Across the stream a small band of men appeared

among trees and through mist. They dressed in light
armor held together by rags, and they were no more
than a dozen. Some were barefoot. They were a lost
scouting party, or adventurers at the end of their adventure. Spaniards afoot in mist that rose from the
hot forest; they looked like a walking museum of mis-
ery. They seemed to consult, argue as in pantomime.
They were insubstantial, but more real than the slid-
ing away, ghostly forms we had earlier seen through
mist. They formed a disjointed line facing the stream.
When Charles fired in the direction of the hillside,
the line of men across the stream took no notice.

We turned to see Charles reloading. A horse
stomped, cried, and Charles spoke to it like one friend
to another. The horse quieted.

"No sense firing," Bester told Charles. "They're
from the past. To them, you're from the future. They
do not see you."

"Movement on the hill," Charles said quietly. "I
shot as a warrant in case anything there is living."

"Just like that Spaniard across the stream who let
off a random shot," Bester muttered. "He tried to
scare the men who are going to kill him."

From the hillside savages appeared and they were
as spectral as the Spanish. They cavorted and jeered.
They tumbled down the hillside in a mob, not seeking cover among trees. They gathered near the banks
of the swollen stream, actually prancing. They seemed
an unlikely war crew of old men and boys. The savages carried clubs, staves, short spears. From across
the stream came another puff of smoke, but no savage fell.

"Can't hit the back of a barn." Ephriam probably
said it, but all thought it.

"Old Indian trick," Bester said about the cavorting Indians. "They draw attention to themselves. The

real war party will come in from behind. Watch what happens in yonder forest."

From the forest behind the Spaniards, movement in mist became warriors. These were no cavorting savages, but skilled men. They moved upon the Spaniards with stealth, then fell on the backs of surprised men. They clubbed and they used stone knives.

The Spanish turned to their enemy. Lances thrust, swords flashed, and not in vain. A warrior fell, and then another. Faint cries echoed through mist. The Spaniards were overwhelmed, clubbed backward toward the stream. All but two died of wounds. The other two drowned.

"What happens if we fire into that fuss?" Ephriam had finally turned from the hillside.

"Nothing," Bester told him. "You can't change history, only put up with it. It's like a blasted play. Acted over and over. Century after century." He turned away. "Move out. There's no sense watching what's going happen to those corpses."

We turned quickly aside. During the war all of us had seen dismemberment, and worse. I thought of my own savagery during the war. I was only a little less savage than those ghostly warriors, now hacking away with stone knives. We departed that scene of ancient carnage.

......

Over the next ten days, and eighty westward miles, we spoke little and observed much. Harness, which had been well-oiled, began to squeak for want of care. We were never exactly wet, yet we never felt completely dry. For awhile, even Bester was puzzled. A pattern emerged. We would see a congregation of spirits, especially soul-catchers. We, or rather Bester, would sense the presence of raiders. We would tether our horses and take positions of defense. Movement would begin in the forest. We would witness battles through mist. Indians, whites, Africs. Whenever ghostly battles appeared, living raiders disappeared.

"Those gents are molded, but never baked hard," Bester said about the raiders. "It's usual."

Since the war, scattered bands of men roam the south. Known as raiders, they are also marauders. They are mostly former soldiers who know about murder, but know little about soldiering and nothing about honor. They are cowards, scamps, violators of women, and burners of cabins and settlements. They will not go face-to-face with a real man. They are backshooters.

"It's not something that's just-minted," Bester told us. "In these hills it's gone on since always. Only the Almighty knows how long."

Before the war, and even now, Indians raid back and forth. They steal women and children, and they kill. Revenge and murder and low deeds are not exclusive to armies.

"But what's baffling," Bester said, "is how the enemies keep changin'. We get half-cooked whites and negras, then we get maverick Cherokee. The only common bond is cowardice."

After ten days we had seen enough to understand that we progressed through history. Spectral Spaniards gave way to spectral Englishmen, and Indian weaponry now included bow and arrow. Then Indians obtained guns. Flintlock pistols appeared. Africs came onto the scene, as slaves, or as adventurers, or raiders. Sometimes we did not witness a battle, but an assassination. Sometimes we saw small settlements burned, or single cabins despoiled. Weapons continued to improve. Woodsmen carried Kentucky rifles which were flintlock, but no longer smoothbore. When cap-and-ball rifles appeared, we became uncertain.

"I already sailed through hell. I'm damned if I want to walk through it." Ephriam said this to Charles, and Ephriam's words sounded like an accusation.

We were suddenly more afraid of each other than of any enemy. We made camp when the sun already stood in back of the hills. Charles tended the horses in declining light. Nobody said a word about losing horses, but the trail was playing out. I privately thought "good riddance." The horses had grown thin and weakish. Only the mule prospered.

Somewhere ahead the trail would narrow and then disappear. I supposed Charles already felt the loss of horses.

"You may get a second helping of hell." Bester knelt above a small cooking fire. He looked toward the horses. "We're walking into something. If the trail was still useful it would be open. Something mighty dead lies westward."

"Talk this out ahead of time." Charles had followed Bester's lead, but now he tried to take charge. "Weapons keep improving. History closes in. We'll soon relive our own sorrows."

I had not thought, when agreeing to this adventure, that I would have to relive the War of the Rebellion. Now three Yankees and a Reb walked toward their recent pasts.

"Get it sorted before we have a spat," Bester told him. "Gravel in your craw. Spit it out." Bester still knelt before the fire, but he suddenly seemed tuned to action. Our rifles were stacked, but our revolvers were right at hand. Bester spoke quietly, as bespeaks a confident man.

"Start with this," Ephriam said, and he was equally quiet. "Why would a man of your complexion stand with the Confederacy?" Ephriam always signals his willingness to fight with a small laugh, as though indifferent.

"And why in the name of Old Ned would a man of your complexion march into a another man's house, and burn it?" Bester's anger sounded dangerous. He shifted his weight, but lightly. His position changed and he could now get at his sheathed knife, as well as his revolver.

"I understand," Charles said. "Men defend their homes. We all understand that."

"You understand horseshit," Bester told him. "I had a place. Had to kill a man to get it."

"Not original," Charles said easily. "We've all killed more than our share."

"Difference is," Bester said, "the gent I killed thought that he owned me. I even owe him somewhat. I even halfway liked the bastard. He brought me up as a house nigger."

And that, I thought, explained why Bester, when he wished, could act like a southern gentleman.

Bester was not done with Ephriam. "Your sojer boys burned me out. Be glad for them that I had nor chick, nor child, for I would have tracked them even after I sent them to hell. As it was I left three rotting in the weeds." Bester paused. He was clearly trying to hold his temper. "So why does a man of your complexion come barreling into another man's business?" he asked Ephriam. Then Bester turned to Charles. "Are you forgivin' me? Because don't. I'm not particularly forgivin' you."

"Forgiving is for priests. Don't get me started on blackbirds and their rosaries." Charles actually chuckled, and that broke some of the tension.

"You were in the goddamned Navy," Bester said to Ephriam, "and you're ready to talk to me about slavery?" He sounded more peaceable, like he too was about to laugh. Then he did laugh. It was a harsh laugh, but allowed space for argument.

And Ephriam, who is no fool, saw the foolishness of anybody ever trying to enslave Bester. And, Ephriam thought of the Navy; of filthy rations, flogging which was supposed to have ended in 1844, scurvy, and death so slow and painful that hanging would be a mercy. And Ephriam also laughed. A little. Tension began to abate, but all of us remained aware of weapons kept handy.

"There were no statesmen," I told them. "There were soldiers, and villains, and slave holders and Massachusetts industrialists, and bad generals and bad politicians and stupid presidents. We four were soldiers. Don't shove politics or memories onto each other." For once I was glad for my size and strength. Big men can command attention if they wish.

"Soldiering," Charles said. "We were all good at it. Hold on to that. Put memory on the shelf."

Easier said than done. Soldiering means battles, and battles mean unspeakable acts. In battle, all of us had cursed some of our fellows even as we cursed the enemy. All of us had fought beside men we loved and respected, but we had also fought beside men so foul and wild-eyed that the only cure for them was a Minie ball. Not all death in battle is caused by the enemy. An army cleans its ranks of certain kinds of filth.

As tension eased a thought occurred. I knew the quality of my comrades. Any fight between us would be face to face. At least no one had to worry about turning his back. A good deal of respect came with the thought, and a good deal of comfort.

And so we had avoided a fight, but we had not avoided suspicion between ourselves and Bester. We trekked for three more days. Black smoke rose from valleys. We heard the roll of drums, and distant Thunder. Cannon echoed through the valleys. I kept thinking of the young boy I'd killed. During the war I had seen things so obscene that the mere killing of a lad seemed pale. The difference was that I had seen those things, but not done them; well, not exactly; well, not all of them.

But, I had killed the boy. I had watched his eyes, had seen startlement and fear when he looked at remnants of his hand. I had felt his skull crush beneath my blow. Pondering, I forgot to pay attention. I cannot imagine allowing myself to be so stupid.

Toward sunset we unsaddled nervous horses in a grassy glade. From the forest came crashing of a heavy body. Somewhere ahead lay an end to the trail. We feared what we would find. I, who was comforted by the crashing sounds in the forest, was surprised when we were attacked.

"Soul-catchers are about to make a catch." Bester yelled as he sought cover.

Charles and Ephriam grabbed rifles and headed for shelter among trees. Mud exploded between the legs of my horse, and the horse jumped sideways and shrieked. The horse banged against me, and mud from the shot splashed my leg. I held the reins, and staggered like a drunken man while fumbling for my rifle. Then I fell and rolled. Charles had one horse on long tether, one on short. Two horses fled. The mule cried, stomped, became crazed and would actually have rolled, but Charles ran to it. He used it as shield while he calmed it and secured its lead. From the forest across the glade came whoops and hollers, but not the whoops of Indians. These were renegade white.

"Take our front," Bester told Charles.   To Ephriam he said, "Drift to the left."   He moved quickly to the right and into the forest, silent as a ghost.   Ephriam shrugged, gave a low laugh, and looked almost happy.   He rolled to the edge of the glade and found thin cover behind leggy rhododendron.   I turned from the yells and covered our rear.

The glade was a circle of grass.   I wagered to myself that yells from across the glade were another trick, and that attack would come from behind us.   I would get first shot.   I got the second.   Bester's rifle sounded.   From cover a man rose, staggered, fell, flopped around for a moment and lay quiet.   He was red-haired and wearing dirty linsey-woolsey now flushed with blood.

My shot caught a second raider in the face.   A 45-70 is a dreadful weapon.   The man's head did not disappear, but most of it did.   This raider wore filthy store clothes, and one could not tell much about him because of the missing face.

Silence.   Yells ceased.   Movement ceased.   From somewhere in the trees came the chuckling call of ravens.   More silence, as if we and the world waited and wondered.   Then ravens flocked above the dead men.   They hovered in trees.

"Thin pickings," Bester said about the ravens.   "They wait for the souls to depart."   He still scanned the forest as he searched for the enemy.

The ravens descended in a flock but did not alight.   They flew in circles no higher than two feet above the dead men.   They called as they flew, and then, dropped.   They covered the corpses.   I could swear, and I am not a mystical man, that the dead man with the red hair uttered a curse.   His lips moved, his dead eyes rolled as sounds of crashing came from the forest.

Then Thunder exploded, not from the west but

from above. Thunder boomed stronger than massed artillery. It pounded onto the forest, and the very side of the hill trembled. Thunder rolled about valleys and hollows, and wind rode the Thunder. Wind rose among trees, and small branches flew all around. Yet, there was no rain.

Sunlight pinioned the dead men across the stream. Wind moved red hair of one, blew against blood and gore of the other and tore at clothing. Ravens rode the wind as easily as kites on a breezy day. Then they rose with the wind and disappeared over the forest.

Wind wrapped around us and forced us to ground. Sunlight seemed brighter, and where there should have been rain, and should have been lightning, there was only Thunder. We yelled to each other through crashes of Thunder, and our voices were like spirits calling across distance, like echoes across time.

And all of it happening in sunlight. When Thunder stopped as quickly as it began I found myself lying not far from Charles. The tethered horses were crazed. The mule stood drooping, beyond madness, broken and stunned.

"Good shooting," Bester said, and I did not know whether he spoke of his shot or mine. "Pretty good dust-up." He emerged from the forest and stood beside me. He looked toward Charles, looked at the horse. "I figured," he told Charles, "we'd end up trading horses, not losing 'em. Let's chew this over." He watched forest across the glade while I watched forest behind the dead men. "I heard six men," Bester said. "We got the two who weren't yelling. There were eight, all told."

"Free the remaining horses, keep the mule." Charles did not like what he was saying, but then, Charles is fond of horses. "Better the raiders have them than they fall as prey." The horses were domes-

ticated beasts. They were unlikely candidates for life
in a forest of predators.

It made sense. The trail was playing out. If raiders had horses, they would have to go back along
useable trail, not forward.

"Strip all gear and cache it," Bester said. "Make it
plain what you're doing. We'll lay a trap." Bester gave
a low laugh, and it was neither humorous nor kind.
"Somebody will get the horses, never fear." He continued to watch the forest. "Thunder," he said, "that's
what the old woman sent. That god-blessed bear *is*
Thunder."

Charles calmed the two remaining horses. We left
them unhobbled in the glade. It's a tribute to Charles
that they grazed, because a short time before they had
gone mad.

We cached saddles and harness, tossed saddlebags
onto the mule, then trekked into the forest. We walked
for a good half mile, then tethered the mule and
turned back.

"One volley," Bester said. "That's all we'll get."

By the time we returned to the glade two raiders
sat astride our runaway horses. The man in command
was well groomed compared to four others who were
at the cache retrieving saddles. The commander sat
his horse in the style of an aristocrat. Although he
was not a large man his presence was forceful. He
dressed in brushed gray coat and clean trousers. He
gave quiet orders that were obeyed immediately. I
thought at the time that it would be of some note to
kill this silken gentleman. In these wet forests it
seemed that one mostly killed riff-raff.

The two men Bester and I had shot lay like discarded rags. They were ignored by the living raiders.
Since the departure of the ravens the corpses looked
shrunken. The red hair no longer glowed. It looked

bloody-brown.

We took cover at the edge of the forest. We had a clear view of the glade.

"Take the horseman on the right," Bester whispered to me. To Charles and Ephriam he whispered, "on my signal." When he was satisfied that all was in place he gave the command to fire.

Both horsemen were dead before they hit the ground. The leader's chest exploded. He jolted up and back. Some dying instinct flung him backward as he tried to clear stirrups he didn't have. The horses wheeled and once more ran. The second corpse lay trampled. Two men at the cache, shot by Ephriam and Charles, had been carrying saddles. They staggered beneath the heavy bullets: .45 caliber, 70 grains of powder. They fell, then one tried to rise and run. Charles finished him off, while the other gasped blood and then lay motionless. Two other men fled into the forest.

"Prayers do get answered," Bester said. "I got to figure that nearby, some women have been prayin' for widowhood." He rose and spat toward the corpses, then walked away without a second glance. Ravens chortled in the distance. I took satisfaction in hearing them.

We trekked for another day and then the trail played out, but not the way we had supposed. We found ourselves on a high ridge looking into a barren valley. In the midst of mountains covered with dense forest, we viewed naked ground. Smoke from fires showed where downed trees still burned, and a clear stream turned into a dark flood as it rushed through the valley. Stench of putridity rose on a breeze. The remains of a broken cabin lay scorched beside the stream. At the head of the valley another cabin sat gutted and smoking. This had once been a settlement.

Guns lay tumbled, and bodies in ragged gray lay scattered. Bodies dressed in sturdy blue lay in waves across the face of the hill. We walked toward a battle-field of a too-familiar kind.

"...difference between spirits and ghosts..." Bester whispered. "You can generally smell the ghosts." For the first time since we met Bester we saw him hesitate. He probably tried to guess our minds, as we were trying to guess his.

After losing the horses and killing six raiders, I hoped any differences between us were past. We had stood beside each other in battle. We had relied on each other.

"This is the past," Charles murmured. "Hang onto that, gentlemen. It's been said and done."

"Agreed," Bester told him, "but we walk through it, not around it." He looked west where a sky dark as ravens was cut by hot streaks of light, and illumed by orange glows of fire. "Not because we want," Bester added, "But I figger there's no god-blessed avoidance."

We descended into the valley, and we were as heavily laden with memory as the mule was laden with gear. The animal grew increasingly skittish, though broken of spirit. It still walked well. A well-found mule is one of the strongest of living creatures. Some even have character.

I remembered thinking that if we moved toward the future, nothing the future would have to show would be worse than walking through this valley. Then I wondered how, if ghosts of Spaniards could not see us because we were their future, could we see our future in that orange-glowing west? For a dazed moment I had the sense that we not only walked through the past, but toward it. And that made no sense.

Dead men and dead horses lay all around. Stench

covered the battlefield like a blanket, and small animals moved among the dead. We walked with care. Grotesque faces, men and horses, broken and twisted limbs, even oddly fashioned deaths... one cannoneer leaned against a blasted stump, and his death had not come from shot. A piece of wood pierced his throat, wood exploded from his cannon's carriage.

As if mesmerized we followed the blackened stream. The mule seemed ready to bolt. The stream tumbled around corpses, and even the running water carried stench. When we passed the first broken cabin I looked inside and wished I had not. A man's head peered with ivory-blank eyes. Only the head. Long-haired. Teeth curiously shiny, the lips more smile than grimace. The body had been exploded.

Charles grunted like a man hit. Bester snarled. Ephriam made no sound. I recall thinking that we were passing through the worst of this particular battle. The going would get easier.

The going did not, and I wish that a clear record of this part of our adventures did not have to be made. We passed the depth of the valley where the stream curved away and ran toward a distant river. At the bend sat the other cabin we had seen from the ridge. This cabin had not been under direct fire from the battlefield.

As we approached we heard tiny cries echoing from the cabin. We knew full well that we dealt with specters, yet the cries sounded authentic. We had to look.

A corpse lay beside the doorway. It was dressed in rough and torn garments. A rusty pistol still lay in its outstretched hand. This was the remains of a settler, a three-for-a-penny farmer.

Bester stood above the corpse. "You ignorant fool," he said to the corpse. "You should have taken your folks and fled. You doubly-dammed fool. Did you think an army wouldn't pay its respects?"

Charles stood in the doorway. "For his sake," Charles said about the settler, "I hope he died first."

And Ephriam, whose experience had been limited to men killing each other at sea, leaned against the door post. Ephriam knew about dead men but not about land warfare. He looked sick. Then Ephriam walked away to stand beside the stream. He stared into the sky, like a man looking for a God that he could curse.

In the cabin a girl of ten or eleven lay naked, broken, obviously raped. She had been barefoot and one ankle was twisted, broken, and she had thus suffered greatly. She had then been murdered by knife and scalped.

A young woman, also raped, lay disemboweled with her foetus torn from her belly. A small boy lay with his skull caved in beside an old woman who had been bayoneted. Her blood lay like a thin carpet across the dirt floor of the cabin. In the old woman's arms lay another boy-child of perhaps two years. It had crawled to the arms of its dead grandmother. It wailed, and the cry was weak from starvation and want of water. Its eyes were crusted and closed. Thus had it lived the last days of its short life, thus had it died.

"Cherokee don't scalp," Bester murmured. "Your northern boys bagged themselves another Confederate." Bester knelt for a moment before the torn foetus. It was almost a child. The eyes were formed. It had rudimentary fingers. "Brave men. Brave men. A young nation's pride." He walked away from us, and did not say another word for the rest of that ugly day. And we had nothing to say to him.

But Ephriam had something to say to me. He drew me aside. "I reckon that was unusual?"

"No," I admitted. "A man could wish that it was."
"T'wasn't manly," he said. "Don't mention that, and manhood, in the same breath." And, from then on, Ephriam barely hid his disgust for us.

III

Strikes of light grew frequent as we moved west. Trees usually shattered and smoked, but sometimes the air only sizzled with heat. Thunder walked nearby in the shape of a bear; or so Bester claimed.

We saw amazing changes in weapons; new smells to the stench of battle, new shapes to the sounds of war. Smells of burnt powder grew sharper. Smoke from cannon and rifle turned pale and gray instead of thick and cloudy. Cannon no longer gave flat reports. Cannon cracked sharp as a slap on the face of the world.

Stench of the dead remained the same. Razorback hogs still fed on corpses, while raccoons and rats competed with the hogs. The battlefields were hurryscurry with movements of feeding beasts.

We skirted battles, but might have walked through the middle of them. Ghostly weapons exploded, and ghostly men fell. We walked unharmed, except in our dreams.

Ephriam kept to himself. During the war Ephriam had ordered the corpses of comrades, or pieces of corpses, tossed over the side after battle. He had directed men as they drew sea water and washed gore from decks. But, he had never seen raping of children and the murder of babies. When he spoke at all, Ephriam spoke to Bester. He treated Charles' mild suggestions as unwanted orders, and scarcely honored Charles with a reply. He treated me as an accomplice. I did not respond. I had my own troubles.

We felt immersed in new weapons and old miseries. We at first believed we heard one of the new Gatling guns. When we finally identified the weapon we found it was far smaller than a gatling, like artillery reduced in size. It sprayed shot too quickly to count.

"We have surely passed into the future." Charles said this as we camped beside a stream. August heat had given way to September mist. Westward, the sky glowed with fire and sundown. Surrounding mountains already lay darkened, the mountains still verdant but with trees in beginning change. We had progressed well and game remained plentiful. The mule proved sure-footed but weakening. It was a large, black animal with a hide that had once glistened in the sun. Now its flesh was thinning, its spirit broken. We lightened its load. We kept all of our salt and tobacco, a little coffee, a little tea, and most of our ammunition.

"I recollect one evening," Bester said, "when our boys sat at a fire like this and admired the better shooting of the enemy." Bester hunkered before the fire. His dark face seemed to absorb and reflect, at the same time, the fire-glow. He whetted his skinning knife on a pocket stone. The blade reflected the fire, dull red. "One of the reasons you gents took such pains to lose good men was because you were too disciplined."

"I like a joke same as the next man. Too disciplined?" Ephriam did not understand what Charles and I knew to be true.

"Take a lesson from the raiders," Bester told him. "Never make a frontal attack when you got other ways to jump. If the damned general says t'otherwise, shoot the damned general. Your lads didn't shoot the general." To Charles, he said, "I don't figure we walk in the future. If we do, there's no sense to it."

"It isn't only time, but place." Charles sounded pettish because he had lost control of our party. Ephriam ignored him. I looked to Bester, because Bester was the woodsman. Charles was in no position to argue, but was not ready to concede his notions. "During the late war there were no major engagements in these hills."

"But we've seen them." I, too, was puzzled. "And we see strange and frightening weapons. We see a panorama of war."

"Displacement, maybe." Bester looked at orange glow to the westward. "You early on lost a horse from one of the strokes of light. But ghosts can't see us or harm us. It figures that sometimes we're reading the past, and sometimes the present is reading us." He examined the knife blade, shaved a bit of hair from his arm, and satisfied, sheathed the knife. He pulled from a pocket the small piece of hardened clay and wires that had fallen from the sky, and which he had shown us when we first met. He studied it like a man studies terrain before a battle.

"... somewhere east of Eden in the land of Nod...." As Ephriam muttered he looked at Charles, as though he searched for the mark of Cain. He hunkered beside Bester, and those two strong men looked diminished in the gathering darkness.

"If the future can kill a horse, and strike trees, then it's part of the present." Charles spoke easily enough but he seemed edgy. "If the future can survey us then we're ghosts ourselves."

"As, someday, it seems we will be." I was not entranced with that sort of afterlife.

"We came adventuring." Charles mused to himself. "We came in behalf of ethnology, and now we engage in defeating war." He looked at Bester. "Time is a-whirl?"

"The war didn't braid this nation. The war knotted it." Bester's face was as studied as our own. "Nothing that came before, and I reckon nothing that comes afterward, will get it total unknotted." He rose from the fire and faced the western hills. Thunder rolled in the distance.

"The war deeded an attack on settled ways," Bester told Charles. "War tried to make everybody the same."

"It was war on behalf of commerce," I said. "Northern cotton men wanted to control the supply. Southern growers bound themselves to English mills to lift the price. It was war between men with different ideas about money."

"You boys think the Confederate soldier gave one whoop or hosannah about slavery? You think wrong." Bester seemed to be answering me, but in a way I could not understand.

"I think so," Ephriam said, and he was grim. "Otherwise, why were we fussin'?"

"Things got unsettled," Bester told him. He turned the piece of fired clay and colored cylinder over and over in his hand. "We're in a place where all kinds of men have brought their ways. These hills took them in and changed them, or killed them. Then war invaded. It wanted to missionary us heathens... and still does... make us into little Lincolns and Sumners. Slavery was its grand excuse."

"Damned good excuse."

"No one's denying it," Bester told Ephriam. "There were white slave holders, and negra slave holders, and Indian slave holders. But that's not the point." Bester then spoke directly to Charles. "Maybe you actually do want to learn about folks and not change 'em. If true t'would be refreshin'."

"Unsettled," Charles said. "The ancient tries to preserve, and the future tries to overwhelm."

"I'd almost wish for more raiders," Ephriam muttered. "At least a man's shooting at somebody who can shoot back."

"You won't get 'em," Bester told him. "Cowards won't walk through what we're about."

. . . . . .

Next morning, and well before sun rose above the hills, the mule turned up missing. Ephriam had hobbled it with rope, and Ephriam's sailor-knots do not slip unless he wills it.

"Maybe I mistook about raiders. Strayed or stolen." Bester searched a wide half-circle around our camp and found no sign. He crossed the stream and found no sign. An animal that large would have left a track. There was none. For a wild moment I thought the beast had faded and become insubstantial, like mist.

"Who would have ever figured," Bester said, "that a man would mourn a mule." He divided our remaining plunder into lots for pack and carry. Since my strength was large, even if diminished from the long trek, I chose to haul the cartridges. We still had most of them, and they weighed more than enough to make a man mourn a mule.

Then time turned tortuous. Our declining fortunes hovered like night mist. We struck westward at a slower pace, and we found that although we were sure-footed, we were not as agile as a mule.

Since we made slower progress we saw gradual change. Repeating rifles accompanied repeating cannon. Great coils of wire fenced off trenches. Soil exploded upward, and in the midst of explosions men turned to vapor; explosions so hot that not even blood remained. Hand-thrown bombs bounced down hills, or into crevices where rapidly repeating guns chattered in reply. Huge balloons floated high above as men with spyglasses directed cannon fire. Massive machines propelled themselves across the land, but were not steamers. We gazed astounded because the things could move without the use of horses.

"And nothing different except the weapons." Charles probably said it, but all of us thought it. We looked at our own weapons, and were filled with doubt. We became accustomed to sprawled corpses that lay beside every sacrilege man has ever wrought.

And all of it the same except for weapons. Then something changed and our minds recoiled. We heard a buzz, like a water-powered sawmill, but the buzz came from above.

"There's your sky god," Charles murmured to Bester. "Are we believing what I'm seeing."

We stood dumbfounded. as a kite-like apparatus flew above the hills. A man tossed a small object from the kite. It tumbled as it fell, and it exploded near a trench.

"End of the world," Ephriam whispered. "If they can do that, nothing anywhere is safe." He looked at Charles, at me, "Women and children first." He turned away.

Sometimes the panorama changed. Hills faded into the background and it seemed we walked the streets of broken cities. Only the streets remained. They were filled with smoking debris, and, inevitably, the dead: old men, old women, children, pet dogs, while pet cats ran feral; our world, a charnel house.

For a space of many days we trudged forward as if dreaming. Memory turned to vision, and vision performed dramas in our minds. We could no longer tell if what we saw was spectral or real. Worse, we were visited with our most terrible memories. We were no longer as strong as we had been. While sleeping we sometimes woke screaming. When eating, we carefully divided and shared deer liver against illness and scurvy.

In my visions the young boy I'd killed walked beside me like a son beside a father. He offered a name, Tom, and he offered sights he had seen and remembered: He showed me a small, tributary-cruising steamboat a-glitter in bright paint and brass... a one ring traveling circus... a haying. And he remembered a pretty country lass who to me seemed ordinary enough, but to the boy she was the essence of mystery and beauty.

"Why did you kill me?" he whispered.

"Why were you there?"

"I run away to jine up."

"Your folks?"

"Pa got kilt early on. I left, though Ma said don't." He thought back through his scant past. "Her name is Susy," he said about the country lass.

"Pretty name." I lied.

I walked sobbing, and my companions were kind enough not to notice. They dealt with their own visions.

This dream-state occupied us so we scarcely knew how many miles were passed. All we have is the written record, because, of course, I was scrupulous. It looks like this:

"Fifteenth, ninth month. Followed small river five or six miles until it bent south. Went westering approx two miles straight up, and two miles straight down. Spied an amazingly large woodpecker. Hills not as gentle as they look."

"Eighteenth. Sorrow fills camp. Last night each

man woke. Ephriam had watch. We lay in silence for
rest of night, and dog tired all day. Silence of sorrow
worse than sorrow...."

And, of course, I do not understand the meaning
of all that I wrote. How can the silence of sorrow be
worse than sorrow? Yet, it was true when written.

We only knew that we trekked, made camp, slept,
and sometimes woke with throats raw from moans or
choking. September sun could not defeat chill breezes
that began to blow from hollows and valleys. Days
grew shorter. My record of the trek shows that we
walked through most of September, but none of us
remember the passage. I do not even remember making entries. My record shows that I spent some days
thinking only of warm kitchens and cherry pies.

Then we returned to sanity because it seems that
time twisted. At any rate, it gave us something we
could lay a hand on. I know now that Ephriam, wiser
than the rest, brought us out of that fog of memory.
He did not order events, but his awareness that we
were trapped in memory somehow altered time.

We crossed the side of a low mountain where massive trees blocked sunlight from the forest floor. In
parts of these hills pine forests are impenetrable, but
in the presence of these giant poplar and oak the forest lay open as a tended grove.

From the morning mist we heard the crack of a
rifle. A shot exploded in a tree beside Bester, and
Bester fell and rolled for cover. A weapon began to
chatter like a gossip telling tales.

"Two of them, anyway." Bester hunkered behind
a giant poplar. "An outpost, maybe."

The weapon searched through the forest and we
watched, stunned and voiceless as the thing cut down
smaller trees. It hammered, fell to silence, hammered.
We had huge trees for cover, but not enough under-

growth to move without being seen. We were held in place by a weapon that chattered like a devil with ague.

Worse, we had the low ground. From somewhere at our backs, and above, came a roar and not a buzzing. A silver machine flashed above the forest, and an oblong-shaped object fell in the direction of the chattering weapon. Light bloomed in the forest and trees exploded. A bit of bark, flung like shot, caught Ephriam alongside the cheek as he peered around a tree and looked for a target. He brushed away small bleeding, the injury minor but real. Ephriam actually seemed glad. He cocked his weapon and searched the forest. The enemy out there was corporeal, and could harm. And, it could be harmed.

At our backs shouts came from the forest. Then came a second rushing above our heads, and something exploded in the forest. The chattering stopped.

"Got the dumb-shit," a voice yelled from somewhere behind us. We turned.

"They're not shooting at us," Bester said. "They're shooting at each other. Stay low." Good advice, but not needed.

"Okay for the gold-brickin' Air Corps." We heard the rapid approach of many men. We saw the first one just as the voice said, "Boys, we've got infiltrators or hillbillies. Three medium size and a big'un." The voice now sounded almost conversational. To us it said, "Drop the popguns. Do you bastards speak English?"

The man who appeared from the forest was lean, spare, and clothed in brown uniform. He wore a large helmet and carried an odd-looking rifle. The chevrons on his sleeve were small, where the Union's had been large, but they spoke the same thing. The man was a sergeant.

"Fan out," he told the men with him. How often

I got to tell you yardbirds not to bunch up? Two of you cover these guys, the rest cover the perimeter."

"Be cautious," Ephriam said softly, "about who you're calling a bastard. I don't take kindly." He chuckled. Two men had their rifles pointed at him, but they stepped backward.

"Three whites and a nig," one of the men said to the sergeant. "They brought their minstrel with 'em."

"You are overmatched and about to get scalded," Bester said, and his voice was even more quiet than Ephriam's. "You get one chance to leave before I act. Good advice says, 'take it.' " From somewhere in the forest sounded the crashing of a heavy body.

"There ain't nothin' more common than bullshit," the sergeant said. "Swing away."

Wind rose from the west. It started small but grew quickly. Darkness stood like a great cloud behind the wind. In the darkness green glows appeared, then began to strike like green lightning. Lightning flashed above the forest, striking through the wind, although it seemed not to strike trees. It crashed against the ground, and the familiar smell of scorched soil sailed on the wind.

"Bastardly weather." Bester had to yell to be heard. "Name-callin' weather." He turned his back on the rifles and looked into the forest where broken tree limbs rained to the ground.

Wind hit and we staggered. We found that we could not stand, but had to hunker down. Wind put us on all fours and it seemed there was no lee. When we moved behind a tree, wind followed. I knelt and wind ripped at my clothes. I thought the fabric would tear, and I closed my eyes against the wind. Then I shielded my eyes with my hands and peered between fingers. All of us were down, my companions and the soldiers. All except Bester.

He stood, although in such wind it was mortally impossible to stand. He watched the forest, then motioned to us by placing his fingers in his ears. We knew that Thunder would soon arrive. The sergeant and his men did not know.

It came rolling out of the west, and it carried the sound of all the cannon ever fired in all the history of the world. Thunder held darkness in its maw, and darkness seemed a stage on which green lightning danced. Wind swept the floor of the forest, and we lay flat to keep from being carried away. Pressure in my ears was so great that I screamed into the wind and pounding Thunder. Around me men lay balled up, holding their ears, and open-mouthed, showed that they also screamed. They continued screaming for long moments after Thunder ceased.

The cloud of darkness still enclosed the forest, and from the darkness the young woman we had met at the fish trap emerged. She walked without hurry, and with the confidence of complete power. Low light, a green glow, surrounded her. It framed her against the darkness.

Men lay all around, still gasping, and my head ached from the pounding of Thunder. No one reached for a weapon. Our weapons were like toys in the face of such power.

Bester still stood. "Grandmother," he said in a normal voice. "If that's what you want...." He turned to the soldiers. "She just saved your sorry hides. I bid you gents goodbye."

The sergeant and his men rose, and stepping forward, must have stepped across time. One moment they were there, and the next moment they seem to have walked between layers of time, like time was an open door. They simply walked through and disappeared.

"Grandmother," Bester said to the young woman. "It is good that you are here." Then he lapsed into a musical language, part Cherokee, and part something else. Vowels sounded liquid as a running stream, warm as sunlight.

The young woman spoke to Bester. She looked briefly toward us, then turned away. Her look was not unkind. More than anything else, she seemed mildly interested.

Charles, on the other hand, could hardly restrain from questions. He watched as Bester and the woman made signs as they spoke. Their hands moved casually. Bester sounded more comfortable than he had sounded in quite a while.

"Grandmother," Charles whispered. "He called her grandmother, and yet that cannot be."

"Take his word for it," Ephriam snarled. "After all that's happened, take the man's word."

"And is he a man?" I could not explain how Bester could stand in wind so strong that other men had been forced to ground.

"I'm blamed sure of one thing," Ephriam told me. "You can't lick him and I won't. If you're thinking fight, don't think it."

Ephriam had given voice to thoughts I tried to avoid. The war had placed a gulf of fury between us. Anger dwelt deep in all our hearts and bones. We had narrowly avoided a fight when Ephriam asked Bester why a man of his color stood with the Confederates. I remembered when we discovered the foetus ripped from its mother's womb, and the child crying in its dead grandmother's arms. We had wisely said nothing to Bester. And, Bester, equally wise, had not said much.

The gulf was there. We would be fools to pretend it did not exist. We watched as the young woman turned from us without a glance and walked into the forest. She disappeared among the trees.

For a short space we stood voiceless. Then Bester turned. "She tells that all the time that ever was, or ever will be, is happening all the time. What do we make of that?"

I looked around. There were no broken trees, no smells of burning soil, no indication that a skirmish had been fought here. The forest towered above us unchanged and silent.

"She says," Bester continued, "that the hard part lies ahead." He began to collect his gear. He glanced west and for the moment seemed exhausted, the way men look after battle. "I kinda regret havin' tugged you citizens into this."

Charles murmured. "Make camp. Puzzle this out. Get the lay of the land. Start tomorrow fresh." He did not mean to embarrass Bester, but he was clearly trying to regain control of the party.

"I got the lay," Bester told him. "What I don't have is understandin' it." He sounded puzzled. "I think I just stood in a time when no wind was blowin', and you were in a time when wind was. And take a lesson on what happened to those sojer boys." He dropped his gear, sat on his pack, and rested.

"I'd think," I said, "the woman might have warned us before this."

"Listen to the man," Ephriam told Bester. "He may not be smarter, but he's bigger."

"I reckon she just figured it herself," Bester told me. "The old people see time like a circle. This 'all the time that ever was or ever will be is happenin' all the time'... would be new."

"You called her 'grandmother.' She can't be more than twenty-five." Charles, I remember thinking, was more interested in his damned ethnology than in getting out of this fix. Or, maybe he tried to exercise authority. I also remember thinking that I had completely lost confidence in Charles. And how did the woman know that things were going to get worse?

"If time is a circle," Bester said, "then she just steps across the circle. These old people are practical." He sat head down, and weighed with thought he was not ready to discuss. "If she needs to travel she crosses the circle and steps into her body when it was young. Try traveling when you're ancient and stove up. What she does ain't nothin' but practical."

......

In the days, then weeks, that followed we walked across a darkening land. We saw fewer battles, but more remains of battles. We saw terrible machines broken and torn. Huge, winged things flashed overhead and screamed, or thundered. Litter of small wires and colorful cylinders became common. They were like the one Bester said had fallen from the sky.

Bester examined a few of them. "T'ain't magic. They're parts of something. Flying machines explain the strikes of light, and I maybe see why we're wanted here."

"Strikes of light must come from lenses, like in a lighthouse," Ephriam said. "Arrange enough lenses and you can cast lamplight seven leagues." He looked to Bester. "That doesn't tell why we're wanted here?"

"I reckon war was moving east, and we're pushing it back. I wonder how far it's gotta be pushed?"

We saw corpses that seemed milled into the machines, like grain ground between stones. It became no longer possible to say which was metal and which was bone. We no longer saw the dead as having once lived.

Overhead, odd looking things flew without wings. They gave sounds of chip, chip, chip and whir above the forest. It was interesting at first. But, we became more and more aware that the final product of war is boredom. We were more concerned with our boots, which were wearing out, than with flight or death.

By the third day of November the orange glow had completely disappeared. A red horizon rose just beyond the next mountain, and silver machines sailed through the sky like bolts of lightning. Strikes of light came from the machines. Sometimes one of the machines exploded in a gush of fire.

Finally, Bester halted our trek. We bivouacked beneath a ledge of rock beside a stream. "We're not robed for winter," he told us. "I reckoned this job would be done by now, but it ain't. Get ready to spend a month."

"A month?" Charles sounded absolutely disgusted.

"Takes that long for tanning."

"We could press on," Ephriam said. "Get it over."

"I've been told what we oughta do." Bester looked west. "Beyond yon hill we'll get into the thick of it. We'd need robing, even t'was midsummer."

"The old woman told you. You're under orders?" Charles' disgust now included the old woman.

"I'm under good advice," Bester told him. "If the old woman says robe, we robe. I'll try to discover beaver, but trust in deer. We'll build dead-falls if we must."

"If a man can build boats," Ephriam told Bester, "he can build shelter. I'll put together a pole cabin." Ephriam actually sounded eager. After the uncertainty of the long trek, he now had a job that fitted.

"You aim to tan hides?" I knew nothing about tanning, except that it smelled like Satan's armpit.

"We got a little salt, lye from wood ashes, and we

can use the brains of deer for tanning. Don't know
why that works, but the old folks use it. I'll bring in
the game."

"Bear," Charles said. "Bear is warmer."

Bester looked toward the forest and actually
grinned. "You wanta try? Better study on it." To me
he said, "Build drying racks and a big circle of fire
rings. Weather ain't with us." To Charles he said,
"Take charge of fish. I'll show you how to build a
fish trap." Bester spoke most pleasantly.

Charles, on the other hand, went silent and angry.
Charles could walk through the blood of battle, but
turned squeamish before the gutting of fish. Either
that, or the job was beneath him....

Back during the war, when bivouacked between
battles, men became ill. No one got sick in battle.
After battle, though, and when men let down, disease
stalked the army as a vengeful presence. And, the
moment we let down, it stalked us.

First Charles, then I, fell like men slain before the
hand of disease. Charles lay rolled in blankets, gasping like a man in the final stage of consumption. I
held out for three more days, illness grasping toward
me. I weakened while hauling stones for fire rings.
Ephriam built a cabin, using the cliff and ledge as a
back wall. I pulled in massive amounts of wood, and
told myself to conquer the disease. Then, in spite of
all effort, I collapsed; racked with choking and nigh
breathless.

A blank space exists in this record. I grew hot,
then cold, and lay wrapped a-tremble in blankets. I
recall babbling, calling the names of women long ago
betrayed, of comrades long dead; and I talked to remembered faces of men I had killed.

Charles the same. Charles babbled the names of
horses, and he called to the memory of his mother in

the same way he spoke to horses. Sometimes his mother was a horse, or so it seemed in his mind. Sometimes Charles cursed. Unusual, because Charles does not curse. Yet, when I gained a few lucid moments I heard him out-swear a sailor. And it seemed, he too, had betrayed loved women, but done even worse with women; and had murdered prisoners. In my delirium I wondered if what Charles babbled was true or only make-believe.

We owed our lives to Ephriam, to Bester, and to Indian medicine that Charles had traded for back in August. Ephriam and Bester were heroic. They kept a stout fire going, night and day. They forced bitter medicine down throats that tried to close. When we fought against the medicine they forced our jaws open. Ephriam spoke to us, crooned to us, even joked to us. When I was so dazed that a comfortable slide into death held certain beauty, Bester pummeled me, insulted me, invited me to be angry at him; enough anger to propel me back into life.

The illness crested, fever broke, and I began feeble movement within the small cabin. Ephriam did not speak as kindly after my illness, as during. No doubt I had babbled things best left unsaid.

I had lost the date. "How many days?" I asked Ephriam. And he said, "Too many. Maybe ten all told."

Thus, while time might move all around us, my sense of time become provisional. Entries start with apologies, as for example: "18th day 11th month, or perhaps the 17th, and certainly no more than the 20th, 1879...."

Even worse, time grew frantic. It jumped like Mexican beans. We heard the soft tramp of horses in the forest. We heard the cries of men; commanding, swearing. At other times we saw creatures resembling men, but not fully. And, sometimes, music sounded through the forest, brass bands playing oddly syncopated rhythms, or church choirs singing. At other times, only a great depth of silence.

We recovered slowly. My huge frame seemed to me, thin. For three days I could take little food, and that mostly broth boiled from deer bones. Charles suffered worse. After a week he became able to feed himself, but was not able to walk for another week. When he once more stepped from the cabin an ice-filled wind blew through the forest, and the rushing stream had dwindled. Ice formed along its banks. Snow lay tramped, and showed where Ephriam and Bester had searched for wood.

When I tried to thank Ephriam he said, "Seems like in battle the first man killed is always the ship's doctor. A sailor learns how to make do." His voice was not cordial.

I have always been stronger than other men, and have taken strength for granted. If not Herculean, I could at least pick up and reset a cannon while other men could not. Weakness had been unknown, but now I sat dumbly and scraped hides. I was good for nothing else. The shale scrapers crumbled as I worked; shale a poor substitute for flint. As strength gradually returned I knew I would never again be as strong. I reflected on the difference between humiliation and humility. I am not the first bookish man to have done so.

While Bester and Ephriam worked, time flashed. Sometimes we woke, only to discover dawn turning to dusk. Entire days scampered away, then other days would repeat: the same weather, the same incidents in forest or stream, all of it the same; repeated.

Charles remained close to being invalid. He walked timid as an ancient man stepping on cobblestones. Ephriam cut a stout stick for Charles, and throughout December Charles hobbled.

Christmas came and went. I noted its passage, more or less, but the glorious event failed to inspire. Bester hummed to himself, but it was not a hymn. Ephriam spent most of the day alone in the forest. Charles murmured about Christmas ham.

The New Year arrived. Approximately. The year 1880 did not look promising.

We huddled near the fire as red glow flashed in the west. Snow covered the ground, melted, returned; then came ice. Freezing rain formed on trees and great branches crashed to ground. The stream dwindled further, froze, and we melted ice to gain water.

"A month more," Bester said. "Gain strength. We'll make an end to this in a month." He and Ephriam laced together cloaks using strips of scraped and tanned hide. "Not too tight, sailor," he told Ephriam. "... must be a bit of give or they'll bust."

We sat in the cabin before a small fire. Smoke wound its way along the back wall, up the ledge, and through a trough that Ephriam had hacked from the limestone. "What lies yonder," Ephriam asked. "What lies beyond these hills?"

"Tennessee," Bester told him, "or Kentucky, if north. Due south ought to be Georgia."

"Flatland and big rivers," Charles murmured. "Steamboats. Trains. Commerce. Civilization." Charles' voice held yearning that said, even he, had a bellyful when it came to ethnology.

"Or, maybe not." Bester's dark skin no longer glowed beneath firelight. His fatigue was great, but he only allowed it to show after the day's work. "I won't even declare we're in North Carolina. We should have got beyond these hills a good while back."

"We're in Purgatory," Charles murmured. "Don't

talk to me about North Carolina."

The month passed. Each evening we looked toward the west where red turned to orange, and then orange turned to a sullen combination of silver and blue. Snow and ice covered the forest, but westward looked even colder. Only one noteworthy thing happened. The lost mule either stepped through time, or wandered into camp.

On a cold morning, with silver mist hovering above the stream, the once-vanished mule scavenged thin forage. It was still hobbled, and while we were thin, it was gaunt. The animal's hide was dull and patchy, its withers obviously weak, its ribs prominent.

"Shoot the creature," Ephriam said. "T'will be a mercy."

That was not to be. The appearance of the mule breathed new life, or at least hope, into Charles. "It is my mule," he told Ephriam, "and we'll not shoot it."

"It is your mule," I admitted. "You financed this adventure." I knew Charles well. He would not stay with us much longer. Bester and Ephriam did not see what to me was obvious. They likely thought that when we broke camp the mule would be freed to find its fate.

Charles stayed for one more week, and he spent that week finding forage for the mule. Then, on a gray and silver morning when mist seemed frozen on the mountaintops, Charles spoke to Bester. "We'll break camp, trek south into Georgia."

"We'll not," Bester told him, and Bester was calm. "We have a duty."

"I have a duty," Charles said, and he sounded plaintive. "My belly has digested enough roots and venison and varmints. I've got a duty to get warm and clean." He looked toward me. "And ethnology can go to the Devil."

"Take a robe," Bester told him. "Don't catch a chill." He turned away in disgust.

"Go on," Ephriam told Charles, "Ride all the way to hell if that's what's pleasing to you."

I had nothing to say. I could only wonder if a Yankee headed south was a lesson to the mule, or to Georgia. The last I saw of Charles was his thin figure astride a starved animal that plodded southward. He was, after all, a man who loved horses.

IV

With Charles departed, a sense of ease, or even accomplishment filled our camp. Ephriam did not whistle or jest, but he no longer seemed displeased with every word I spoke. Perhaps my choosing to stay, rather than fleeing south, caused Ephriam to see me as separate from Charles.

"Pitiful," Ephriam said, and looked in the direction Charles had taken.

"He was capable during battle," I told Ephriam. "He was an officer, I a gunner." That was as much explanation as I was willing to give.

Thunder rumbled from the east. Without our noticing, Thunder had moved from west to east, and now it urged us toward the west. If we had thoughts of retreat, we could forget them.

Westward the orange sky had long ago faded, and the sky now glowed in tones of blue and silver that made one think of ice. Charles might fail his duty, but we could not fail ours. At the same time, one could not help but shiver when looking west.

For two more days we paused because Bester balked. He seemed undecided, although he did practical things. He cleaned his weapons. He rolled and unrolled his pack as he decided how much he might carry. Bester was so meticulous that anyone could see he delayed while making up his mind. Finally, on the second night, he decided.

We huddled in the cabin. We had used extra skins lashed with rawhide to cover outside walls. They attracted varmints but protected against wind. In this early February, with ice skimming the land, the skins did not stink. Warmth inside the cabin was seductive. We did not relish a trek into winter.

"We leave Thunder here," Bester began. His brow wrinkled. Firelight softened his dark skin but the wrinkles were shadowed and black. "No. Thunder leaves us." He hesitated. He did not want to say what he knew he must say. "Beyond yon ridge we leave everything: forest, old woman... I know not what else."

"The old woman told you?"

"We can choose to see this through together, or we can go our separate ways. As near as I can figure, we're looking at a different kind of battle."

"We've come this far together."

"Problem is," Bester told me, "there's weight between us. We got to get it settled. We got to be together in fact, as well as name...."

"The war is over."

"You're dreamin'," Bester told me. "North will never respect the south, and south will never get done despisin' the north. The war will never get over."

"I didn't burn cabins," Ephriam said. "I helped burn prizes to the water when we had no prize crews left. I fired on blockade runners. I killed men, but I never burned no cabin." It was not exactly an apology.

"If the war is never over, why in the name of Old Ned are we talking?" I didn't challenge Bester. It was an honest question. "You soldiered," I told Bester, "and I soldiered. I don't know what you did, and you know damn-all about me." I looked to Ephriam. "And you don't know either."

"You told tales whilst sick." Bester was grim.

"You were present at the telling, but not the happening. You weren't there."

"Damn good thing."

"What tales might you have to tell?" I asked.

They sat quiet, and they thought. For the space of some minutes neither spoke.

"I can see how a man might have had his reasons." Bester yawned, but the yawn was forced. He pretended he didn't care. "You in or out of what comes next?"

"I'll think about it," I told him, then paused. The other choice was to go it alone. That seemed awful. "I'm in. Someone has to watch over you gentlemen."

Ephriam chuckled. "In," he told Bester. "If only to view the show."

. . . . . .

Thunder stood at our backs like an encouraging hand. We left the cabin and most of our equipment. We walked heavily robed. We carried light packs, bedrolls and weapons. For the moment, Thunder seemed a friend, or at least an ally. It rumbled like a giant clearing his throat as we climbed to the western ridge.

A tortuous climb. Once, in the long ago, I could lift cannon. Now it seemed almost impossible to place one foot before the other. My boot soles were thin as paper, my breathing shallow and forced. If it had not been for the strength of Thunder, I could not have pressed forward. My comrades the same. Ephriam huffed and puffed. He had lost weight and

was no longer shaped like a barrel. Even Bester
seemed thin. He led, but slowly.

Once on the ridge we looked down onto a landscape of a thousand smokes. Sunlight pierced gray
mist, was swallowed by mist. Chill rose through the
sunlight like the cold of a grave. It was enough to
make the strongest heart turn back. Sunlight funneled
into mist, like milk in a churn.

Struggles went on down there, but of what kind
and quality I could not say. It seemed that smokes
from not a thousand, but many thousand fires rose
black through silver mist. Although cold rose from
the valley, red flashes glowed hot as anthracite.

I thought of turning back and dismissed the
thought. I could not fail Ephriam and Bester. Then I
told myself to be honest. The long trek down to an
empty cabin seemed more awful than being swallowed
by mist.

Our descent produced layers of dread. If Thunder had not mumbled like a sleepy animal, the descent would have been impossible. Thunder then
faded, and was gone.

"We're on our own, gents," Bester muttered. "I
figger we're headed to a place where no one rules."

Dread arrived during the first thousand yards. We
did not know where we were, but it was certain it was
not the Great Smoky Mountains. Or, anywhere else
frequented by living man. Of the dead, though, there
were a-plenty.

"A cloak, a cloak." The voice quavered like that
of an ancient man, but I saw no man. At the same
time, the voice sounded familiar, if haunted. Ephriam
turned, bewildered, looked all about. Bester shook
himself, like a dog shaking water from its coat. He
looked confused, and Bester was never one to be confused.

The voice rose from a scorched landscape and the voice surrounded us. I feared I would actually breathe it in, and tried to slow my breathing. "Poor him's a-cold, poor him. A cloak, a cloak."

Fires burned here and there, and wrecked trees smoldered. Yet, the voice complained of cold. It grew faint as we passed downward. Cold wrapped the side of the hill, a cloak, no doubt, but a cloak that told of ice.

"Trickery, trickery, dickery, dee...." It was a child's voice. A waif skipped past singing. She stopped and turned. "Me lights was blowed out an' I no longer see." She was blind. And skipped.

Bester sobbed. Caught his breath. Choked. I could see no reason for it, but he momentarily slowed.

"Mad?" I questioned about the child.

"Lunatic," he said, but spoke not of the child.

Then a woman's voice. It murmured through mist, and then it wept. And then it rose in anger. And then retreated once more to murmur. Betrayal seemed to live in the air, and I remembered women, and the promises I had once made. And broken.

This voice I could not remember. All I could understand was its immense grief, and from that I recoiled.

"I'm not understanding much," Bester said, his voice subdued. "But this is a time like no other time. Like a time that time forgot."

"I feel almost alive. At the same time, fairly-well not." Ephriam pulled to a slow halt. He studied. "All the time that ever was is happening all the time?"

Beneath our feet smoke drifted from burned soil. The stench of death was replaced by the stink of burning peat, yet frost covered the ground. From the gray and silver mist came the sounds of water breaking against a shore, a distant rush of water.

"If you wish to return to life," the woman's voice whispered to us, "do not falter. Retreat is an acceptance of doom." The voice carried little hope, and no trust.

I could not tell from wither the voice came. And what did she mean, "return to life"?

Ephriam made a decision on the strength of that voice. He walked toward the sounds of breaking water. We followed, and we advanced toward a distant shore. Low surf murmured as we walked. An iron gray sea swelled around rocks, and not far offshore a barkentine carried torn sails. Fire climbed the aft mast. The vessel rode so low that burning sails seemed to rest on the surface of the sea; a hull about to take its final dive.

A second vessel, a brig, stood close-hauled in a dead calm. Sails drooped and the commission pennant hung lifeless. Men worked to clear decks after battle. They said little: a distant curse floating across water, the cry of a man wounded, the faint slosh of sea water cast on decks to clear away blood. A marksman, rifle slung across his back, climbed to the crosstrees.

"A cloak, a cloak. Poor him's a-cold." The voice came from one of two figures standing before surf. The one that spoke was old and hunched and thin. It trembled as it stood, and its call went across the surf and to sea; and its call went landward. I did not understand how such a feeble voice could cover such distance.

The second figure was equally old, but it stood erect and at ease. It was still muscular and barrel-shaped. I knew before it turned who I would see, and Ephriam knew as well. He also knew who he would see when the thin figure turned. We stopped, stunned and for the moment, voiceless.

"The time that time forgot," Bester murmured after a long pause. "Is that what's happening?" He watched Ephriam as Ephriam watched two versions of himself as an old man. Ephriam grunted, like a man hit. "Uh, uh, uh...." He looked seaward.

Men from the sinking barkentine were in the water, while other survivors rowed two small boats. They attempted to rescue the swimmers. As they approached each swimmer, a rifle sounded faint across the swells, and a puff of smoke issued from the crosstrees of the brig. The swimmer would shake, the water would turn red, and the man would disappear beneath waves. Ephriam groaned.

I looked toward the brig. In the crosstrees the sniper sported. He chose swimmers about to be rescued. His shots moved ahead of the small boats, searching for men, denying life. From the deck of the bark sounded a familiar laugh. Too familiar. Ephriam choked, made odd sounds in his throat. Finally: "I had charge of the deck. I could have stopped that." He unslung his rifle. His face twisted with loathing, but the loathing was for himself. He looked at the rifle as if he tried to understand its use. I thought, perhaps, he would shoot at the man in the crosstrees. Then, for a moment, I feared he would shoot himself. Instead, he threw the rifle from him as if it were a thing diseased.

"It's not a time like you said," he whispered to Bester. "It's a time of choices. It's not a time that time forgot, but a time when I can act like the man I should have been." He looked at the two standing figures; the wailing old man and the stalwart old man. "Do I become old and simple, or old and of use to the world? Gentlemen, I rejoin my ship."

He kicked off his boots and shrugged out of his furs. "Should you chums ever drift downeast to

Maine, and if I'm there, we'll drink and tell tales."

"We'll cover you," Bester said, but sounded doubt-
ful as he unshouldered his rifle.

"Don't," Ephriam told him. "Whatever happens
is what's supposed to." He walked into surf and disappeared, like he stepped through a doorway of time.
When we turned, the two figures of Ephriam had disappeared as well.

"We should have stopped him."

"You know better. Think on it."

. . . . . .

We turned away from the sea, Bester and I, and as
we turned the sounds of surf disappeared. Wails
drifted through mist, and wails were like silver blades.
Hurry and scurry carried on around us, and sometimes we could see movement of men. We could sense
dread, resolve, horror. Mostly we trekked.

Cold days gave way to colder nights and fires
gleamed before crouching men. It seemed we walked
through a bivouac of ghosts and ghostly fires, the fires
burning but cold.

"I'm understanding more than I want," Bester told
me. "I thought the old woman wanted me to take
your party away from the hills."

"She didn't?"

"She did. What I didn't figger was she wanted me
gone as well. She's practical."

"I don't follow."

"Men protect their homes," Bester said, "but it
changes 'em. Once the fracas is over, nobody wants
what they've become... can't blame her for gettin' rid
of me."

"... you've been listening to preachers. I'd think
better of it."

"T'isn't that," Bester told me. "I figger we brought war with us. It would never have moved eastward without us. We drew it like offal draws flies."

"More preacher-business."

"Don't be a fool." Bester sounded about to lose patience. "We can't forgive each other because we can't forgive ourselves. That's what Ephriam discovered. He's forgivin' himself."

Bester peered through mist. Stink from black powder was so ordinary that I no longer smelled it. Stink of fire was common as well, but the stink of burning that lay heavy in the air was like a bonus of sorrow. "I don't know about you," Bester said, "but I'm walkin' into something. Something lies just ahead."

The terrain gave way to rolling foothills where scorched trees leaned toward smoking earth. Camp-fires glowed through mist and through night, but the fires were small compared to what we saw and smelled from the distance.

The horizon was alive and red with fire. As we progressed Bester began to tremble. "What you'll see," he whispered, "neither man nor devil would wish." His walk slowed as he thought on his words. "No, a devil might wish it. You could say a devil did... a devil with hell in his heart."

Fire bloomed through and above a cabin roof, and a twin fire bloomed above a barn. A plowhorse stood tethered, having been stolen from the barn. Squawks of fowl swept through the night, while, standing be-fore the fires, a group of soldiers wrestled with a squealing hog. They cut its throat, and before it was dead cut away the hams; were prepared to leave the rest. Firelight silhouetted them as they packed meat into a cotton sack.

Small plunder lay about, skillet and pots. Blue uniforms shone black in firelight. A soldier kicked the hog carcass. "You're emancipated," he told the dead hog. "Oh, Lordy you are free."

A rifle popped from the darkness, and a small tongue of flame leaped, accompanied by a curse. The soldier toppled forward. He fell across the dead hog as if he embraced a lover.

From the darkness came a yell that would curdle blood. It was Bester's voice, and it carried all the fierceness of the Rebellion. The other soldiers fled quick as cats, heading into darkness; all but one who did not avoid a second shot. This soldier was hit low in the spine. He fell forward, and began screaming.

"Satisfactory outcome," Bester whispered. "If only it had stopped there."

What followed was like a magic lantern, a stereopticon. Bester stood beside me. The two of us watched the spirit of Bester ease from darkness into light, then step back into darkness. Flames crackled and sparks rose above the burning cabin like dots of hate. The screaming man moaned, fell silent, then screamed.

We watched as the spirit of Bester once more stepped from shadow, then stepped back just as a rifle shot sounded from the direction of the fleeing soldiers. At least one man remained. The spirit had deliberately drawn fire.

The cabin burned, the wounded man gasped and moaned. For a space of minutes nothing moved, and firelight illumed the corpse of the man lying across the butchered hog. Then, from a distance, the spirit's voice screamed curses. The voice moved further and further away, then fell to silence. For the moment, the lantern show paused.

"I euchred the fool." Bester stood beside me as the sounds of his past disappeared into the forest.

"It was good soldiering." He put a hand on my arm. "I take satisfaction in what happens next. The fool thought I had fled."

From the edge of the forest a shadow appeared. It moved slowly, and as it moved it whispered to the wounded man. "I'm here, Johnnie. I'm comin' to getcha." The soldier edged toward his wounded friend.

The pop of a rifle from darkness, and the soldier folded forward like a collapsing tent. He grabbed at his groin. He screamed. From the darkness Bester's voice spoke, this time quietly, "Like castrating hogs… I reckon you'll sire no more bastards." His voice was lost in the dual screams of the two mortally wounded men.

The lantern show moved. The first paling of dawn gathered above a frame house standing at the edge of a broken town. In dimmest light, shattered buildings stood along a dirt road. From some of the buildings came sounds of weeping. The frame house stood unmarked by battle, and from it came the snores of men.

Beside me, Bester trembled. "Stop it," he muttered, and he talked not to me. Then he turned to me. "I tracked them there. I waited the night. They became drunken."

We watched as the figure of Bester appeared from behind a broken building. The figure carried sacks of black powder and a makeshift torpedo. Bester's spirit moved almost casually, as if it had all the time in the world. It circled the house with a line of powder. When it ran out of powder it made another trip. The torpedo was installed at the front door. It bulked like a dark thought in the growing dawn.

Beside me, Bester groaned. "Seven were there. I'd gotten three. Three should'a been satisfaction aplenty."

Sounds began to issue from the nearest broken building: a child's awakening cry, a woman's hushing voice that was as dark as Bester's skin and as troubled as Bester's furrowed brow. A second child spoke querulous and was hushed by the trembling voice of an old woman. The quiet voice of an ancient man reassured the child.

The family emerged from the building and stood in the gathering dawn. They looked up and down the road, deciding in which direction to flee. The woman was thin, high-rumped with a baby at hip. She was darker than Bester, splay-footed in the way of field hands. The baby was not quite of walking age. A girl of seven or eight stood beside her grandfather and grandmother. The couple stooped, moved with pain, and watched the road as if it would spit forth sorrow. They were a family that had never before traveled ten miles away from home and plantation. A family lost.

The spirit of Bester knelt with flaming torch above a trail of black powder. It watched the family, hesitated, made motion to deal in fire and explosion, hesitated.

The family began to move slowly away from the house and the snoring. Bester touched flame to powder, and a trail of fire encircled the house just as the girl child turned. She ran toward the broken building, for something left behind, a corn cob doll perhaps. She ran toward the fire, and her mother followed screaming. She was still screaming when she and the baby were felled by the exploding torpedo.

The little girl fell, holding her face, rolling in dirt as the two old people hobbled toward her. The old man knelt beside the girl, while across the road flame engulfed the house. Bester ran forward, crazed, and did not go near the child. He stood with rifle at the ready, covering door and windows. One man staggered toward the street and died yelling as Bester's rifle popped. The house burned like hellfire. The lantern show moved.

Bester stood beside me, and held my arm as if he would fall. We watched the little girl roll in the dust and clutch her face. He looked at the lifeless figure of the woman, at the dead baby. "Blinded, and orphaned," he said, but not to me. "Hell of a day's work, and it still early."

"It's past," I said. "You acted a little too fast. A mistake, but it's past."

"It can't be," he said. "It must not." We watched as the scene faded. We stood together on smoking ground. Bester clutched my arm like he was afraid he would fall. There was no strength left in me, or so I thought. I had nothing to spare. Somehow, though, we both stayed on our feet.

Bester shrugged out of his pack. He laid his rifle across the pack, dropped his revolver beside it. "What did Ephriam say? 'Whatever is gonna happen is gonna'?" He looked back the way we had come. I'm backtracking. Somewhere back there I'll come on all this again. Somewhere back there is the man I could have been." He grasped my arm once more. "Go with God's blessing, and go with mine." He paused. "A'course, mine may be a devil's blessing."

"You'll want help. I'll follow."

"I'll want help," he said, and he was grim. "But that's not to be. This gets done alone." He turned from me. "The old woman knew that the only way to defeat war is to defeat it in yourself."

I watched him walk away. I stood and watched for quite awhile, until he faded into distance.

. . . . . .

And then, it was, that my torment began. I had been among comrades for the best part of a year, and now, alone, I felt a different kind of fear. Fear tasted like corroded brass. Fear partly arrived because of weakness. My legs persuaded me that they could not support my pack. For the space of a day, perhaps, I sat beside a cold fire in the same manner that a thousand men sat before cold fires. I chewed dried meat and used my knife to cut away part of my bedroll. Strips of hide from my robe served to bind cloth around my feet. Chill lay all around, and the fire became a mockery of cold.

It was a woman's voice that moved me along. It was a voice of sorrow, of anger, of loss. "Forward," it whispered, "or we are lost."

We? I remembered her not. The voice was not kindly.

A survey of the terrain showed that foothills were lowering. There seemed a promise of flatland, perhaps of fields and easier going. When I stood it seemed impossible to even stagger. Too much weight.

Cartridges weighed heavily in the pack. Without cartridges the weapons were useless. It seemed possible to carry either weapons or food, but not both. I cast the weapons from me as had Ephriam, and Bester.

Hours or days or months passed, or perhaps only minutes. I walked in a haze of thought and memory, but also in clairvoyancy. My mind followed Charles, watched him formally dressed and handing a fine lady into a fine carriage. I saw him standing before a stable of thoroughbreds, and saw his proud satisfaction in ownership. I saw Charles addressing his private club of gentlemen, as he lectured on 'My Solitary Sojourn and Adventures Among Red Men of the Forest.'

Time seemed suspended and I only know that I walked. The landscape changed. Foothills gave way to flat land. Farms abounded with split-rail fences down, barns burned, and the rotting carcasses of beasts dotting farmyards. Field crops stood overgrown in weeds.

Farms gave way to prairie, and I scorned myself for thinking that I once thrilled at adventures told by stalwart Englishmen, conquerors of savages in jungle or desert. Then I thought of a better kind of Englishman, and lines from his poem: *For we are here as on a darkling plain / Swept with alarms of struggle and flight where ignorant armies clash by night.*

But why remember words that spoke of "we"? Charles was gone, and Ephriam, and Bester. The land rolled immense and dark before me. Long grass had been burned, and wind swept fire across the horizon. I walked among cold embers across a flat and dreadful land.

"Find him," the woman's voice whispered. "You dare not falter now."

I did not understand, and I found no one. Fires smoked through the mist and souls wandered. And, it was while I hunkered beside a fire that the boy found me.

"Mister?" His voice came from the mist, and then he appeared. He was as small and frail as a spirit. He still wore the red rag at his throat. His other rags barely covered him, and his torn hand hung limp at his side. He approached timidly. And, although he feared me, I feared him more. "My ma sends me," he whispered. "Looks like we still got dealin's."

A woman's sobs, disappearing.

"Tom," I said. "That's your name?"

"So, 'tis."

"Wrap yourself," I told him. I passed him the blanket from my bedroll. "Are you alive or am I dead?"

"Can't say," he told me. "In these parts it don't

spell much difference." He hunkered before the fire. "You're a growed-up. You're supposed to know."

I watched him and remembered that he had been too brave. In small light from the fire his cheeks were sallow, his hair ragamuffin dirty, and his eyes swollen from weeping. He wiped his nose with a tattered sleeve, squared his shoulders, and pretended he had no fears. In the distance cannon rumbled, or perhaps it was only thunder.

"Bin waitin' for you," he murmured, "...one snakey hell of a long time."

"You're somewhat young to cuss."

"I figgered I was growed-up," he said, and he sounded like he thought he gave an answer. He looked at his torn hand. "I was fixing to be a drummer boy. You could say that part's over."

"I lived in a big city," I told him, "and wrote pieces for newspapers. Then newspapers yelled for war...." I looked over the flat and dying land. "Don't care for that work anymore. You could say that part's over."

From the east, and far away, cannon or thunder rumbled, then diminished. The boy trembled with cold. He clasped the blanket close, and it seemed he yearned toward me. Or, perhaps I only imagined such. I told myself that he had been too brave for a long, long time.

"Ma claims I got to get somethin' figgered. Can't do it 'til I know what 'tis."

"Looks like we both have the same job," I whispered. I thought back on the long journey, the war, the forest, the old woman, the trek. All of it seemed pointed toward a meeting with this child.

I felt a need to touch the boy. Hesitated. Felt the deep fright that he so sternly controlled. No boy so young should have to own so much control. I leaned toward him, then drew him to me. He came willingly.

He snuggled against me the way I had once seen a two-year-old cuddled in the arms of its dead grandmother.

The Englishman's poem kept running in my mind. *...Ah, Love, let us be true to one another....*

It must have been written for a loved woman. Yet, with the boy snuggled in my arms I thought it might well have been written as a father to a son.

"We'll see this through together," I told the boy, as silver light lay cold in the west. "We'll get it figured out. We'll walk together, westward."